Korean Girl

In

America

Hope Kim

***Dedicated to my love, my inspiration, my shooting star*

ISBN-13: 978-1543139990

ISBN-10: 154313999X

Fall

Chapter 1: New Beginnings?

We are once again living in a new area because my mother just ran off with a man and is presently in the process of divorcing another man. I am halfway through the first quarter of my freshman year of high school, and have just been summoned to the principal's office and then told that I must meet with Mr. Morris, who is a political science teacher and part-time counselor. I have heard a little bit about him, but I am not sure why he wants to see me.

I strode into Mr. Morris' office, which was the size of other administrator offices, except for the fact that it looked bigger. There was only a small and sleek desk pushed up against the corner near the only window in the room, with a computer on top and a couple of books stacked neatly next to it.

A thin, cheap-looking computer chair sat right behind the desk. There were no bookshelves, no tables, no diplomas on the walls, or even a picture. It was basically a barren room. The only item which seemed to have any significance was a leather chair which sat in the other corner of the room. It was expensive looking and appeared as if it could fit two people in it, a professor's chair, one you could sit back in with a smoking jacket and a pipe, a glass of wine, and a good book. Just then Mr. Morris entered the room and politely asked me to sit down. To my surprise he grabbed the computer chair and sat right down in the opposite corner, and gestured to me to have a seat in the nice chair. I looked kind of surprised, as if I would be intruding by sitting on the only nice thing in his office.

"Don't worry, *he said*, everyone expects me to sit in that chair because it is the only decent item in this office, but I prefer this simple chair. My wife bought that for me when I first started counseling people, thinking I could sit in comfort, and look more like a psychologist I guess. But I prefer my students to be comfortable."

I scurried over to the chair and sat down with my butt pressing against the front. I wasn't sure if I should look attentive or comfortable, so I chose attentive. By way of background, I knew about Mr. Morris because he was one of the "cool" teachers, and a bit of an enigma. I don't know exactly how old he is, but he looks like he is in his upper 20s or early 30s. He is tall, with dirty blonde wavy hair, and has an athletic body. He has a bit of a baby face, but has a manly jaw line. I picture him as a Swedish tennis player or skier. He definitely doesn't fit the mold of the average high school teacher. People also said he didn't even need a teaching job because he made a lot of money as a trader or stock broker or something like that, and only became a teacher and counselor recently. So he must be one of those do-gooders or maybe a little bit crazy, I dunno.

"It is nice to meet you, Hope. My name is David Morris and I am a counselor at the school when not teaching classes. I have a psychology degree as well as a master's in counseling, which is why I split my duties here. But most of all, I like to help students who are struggling in school or personally. Do you know why you have been sent my way?"

I was already intimidated as he seemed so calm and matter of fact. I wasn't sure whether he was on my side, or against me. Wait a minute…I don't think I did anything wrong, so why is there even a side? "I don't think I did anything wrong, so I guess I am not sure why I am here."

"No, I don't think you did anything wrong either, *he stated*. I have been looking through your file and I believe the thinking is that you are in a new school and your grades are average at best for the moment, but all of your test scores, aptitude results, and grades from your previous schools show you have tremendous talent and ability. So I was brought into this situation to see whether you need time adjusting or if there is something deeper going on in your life which gets in the way of your studies."

I immediately went into some weird defensive mode in my mind and blurted out, "So what is wrong with average grades? I mean, the word average comes from the fact that most people fit into this category, and there are so many people who are below average, and so many average people, otherwise there wouldn't even be the word average, it would be some other word for average and not average." *Ouch, that was painful. What is wrong with me!*

"It is true. While using the word average a bunch of times, *he said with a slight smile,* didn't necessarily help your definition, most people are average."

"So do you see tons of average students in your office every day and try to delve into their averagedom?" *I actually thought it was a good comeback.*

"No, I would not say that I do, *he said with a smile.* If we have a C student who has been pulling Cs all his life, then we do not inquire. Some people are performing at their potential, and some people's potential is average compared to the rest of their fellow students. If a student seems to be underperforming and we pull him into this office but he doesn't want to grow or change, we won't badger him. I am here to give an opportunity to students who want to grow or change, or even just shed whatever baggage or hurt is weighing them down. Sometimes I can be a mentor or friend to students who don't have anywhere else to turn, especially during struggles. I hope I can be that person for you if you would like me to be. But more importantly, I would just like to help you achieve any goals you have in your education and see if there is anything hindering you which you may feel comfortable addressing."

"You mean like my mother? *I spouted out*. Is this going to be some session where we blame my mother from childhood for all of my problems? Maybe you will analyze my dreams and hypnotize me and force me to confront my rage, or have me do a rebirth and start over with my mother, or keep me away from boys who remind me of my father. Or maybe since this is a Christian school all of my problems exist because I don't read the Bible enough, and all the answers are found in the Bible, even the answer to a mathematical proof on an algebra test, or when will two trains collide which are traveling at different speeds from different locations, and Jesus is traveling on one of the trains, so it can go at any speed it wants at any time."

He laughed. "Um, no…to… I think all of your questions. The fact that you already appear to know some forms of psychoanalysis is actually a good start because you are at least open to the notion of psychology but understand the drawbacks. Although I have studied many of the techniques you joke about, I don't buy into many of the theories and techniques which have become so prevalent in the modern world of psychology. A good counselor is like the wise friend, who doesn't seem to exist anymore in our society. This friend would be well-educated and well-read, have steadiness and maturity to confront tough situations, have the ability and gumption to say something unpopular but right, would not crumble under empathy, could challenge but not overwhelm, and be supportive and sympathetic without enabling. I don't think I am there yet, in terms of being the wise friend, but hopefully I am on the path and each student I help gets me closer. I am a believer, so I do look to the Bible for answers, but I see that the world is tough and sometimes we need all the help we can get, whether from friends, family, school, or wherever. The world is sinful and imperfect, and anyone who believes he has the answers to all the ills of the world is, in fact, God. And I haven't seen the second coming so I am pretty sure no one has the right answers all the time, no matter how much he reads the Bible. So I am here to help, and discuss whatever you think is important to discuss. If you don't want to discuss anything and don't want to attend any more sessions, then that's cool with me. If you want to talk about your mother, *he said with a smile,* then we can talk about your mother all day long."

"I know you were just joking then, but seriously, you don't have time to deal with my mother, or my family, or upbringing, or my culture, or race. It would take a session every week for a million years."

"Well, because of the new block scheduling for classes, I have 2 hours 2 times a week for discussions with students. And since I am not counseling very many people at this time, I have two hours once-a-week which I can devote to us if you would like."

Us?... That doesn't sound so bad. Someone devoting time to me without pure obligation? I hope I am not smiling. I need to keep my guard up, though. I mean, the guy seems nice and his answers are soothing to my soul in some weird way, but I can't buy into this yet. "Sounds good, I guess. We'll see."

"Ok, cool, *he said.* We can get to know each other a little bit better as these sessions unfold. So I guess my first question would be why did you move into this area?"

"Ok…um…wow…see…I can't even answer your simple question without going deep. I mean most people would probably just answer that one of their parents took a new job or something. *He just sat there calmly looking at me, sort of inviting me to do whatever I wanted but not shifting topics. Maybe I don't want a new friend, a wise friend as he puts it.* Ok, so…my mother ran off with a guy who she is not married to, she is actually married to another guy, and this new guy is married to another woman, and has kids and stuff, and is totally hiding in a new state with my mother, and I don't know if they know what they are doing. And maybe my stepfather, for lack of a better term, will find us and go crazy on us because he can get kinda crazy, or maybe this new guy's wife will find us and maybe she has a shotgun or something, I dunno. And this new guy is old as dirt anyway, I think maybe in his 50s, and may have a heart attack soon from all of this stress, which is why he plays golf I think, because golf is supposed to relieve stress. And even though he has a given Korean name, he chose Robert as his American name even though his middle initial is 'E' and his last name is Lee. I don't even think he realizes Robert E. Lee was the general of the Confederacy. So me, my mother, and Robert E. Lee actually ran off in the middle of the night, no joke, and drove from Chicago to Michigan with as much as they could fit in the car. My mother left her businesses to run by themselves, or abandoned them. Who knows what Robert left, other than his wife and kids, since I don't even really know the guy. The only time I saw him was actually just a shot of his back-side while he was pulling up his pants and jumping out of our apartment window to the fire escape a few months ago. So now we are holed up in some dirty motel for half the time and my aunt's house half the time, because my aunt wants to support my mother but doesn't want to condone her behavior either, so she is not sure what to do.

Oh, and so my mother chose this school because it is a Christian school, and my family is supposedly Christian. Or maybe it is close to the nearest highway so we can make a quick getaway. Or maybe they think this school teaches its students how to rob trains or banks or stagecoaches like in the movies, in case we have to continue on the run."

"Uh…ok…*he sat there with a bewildered, yet half amused face.* I am trying to speak slowly so I can collect my thoughts. First, thank you for sharing that with me, Hope. I know the humor masks the incredible pain this must be causing you and I think you are brave for even enduring this set of circumstances. There is so much to unpack here so I don't want to get into too much detail right away. But I gather from your statement, and I hope I did not miss something, that this man is not your father, and the man your mother is currently married to is not your father. Since it appears this all happened without your approval, what does your father think about what has transpired?"

"Ok…once again, never a simple answer. My father barely speaks to me. I didn't even know where he was for the last 4 years until he finally reached out to me and invited me to his new place, which happened to be in Toronto. It was crazy to think that my father vanished off the face of the earth, but when he does show up, he is living in another country. So I saw him for a week last summer. We hung out, went to some museums, art exhibits, even Niagara Falls."

"So did your father tell you why he hasn't spoken to you for the last few years or why he moved to Toronto?"

"No and no. I am not sure whether he will ever tell me why he does anything or apologize for anything. It may be his old school Korean belief that parents never really need to explain themselves to their children, or maybe he really is ashamed of some of his behavior but too afraid to admit it. Regardless, I don't think we have the time to delve into his psyche unless you want to be here all day. As far as Toronto, on the surface I have no idea why he is there. He never mentioned a job when we hung out, and since he was hanging with me during the week and his track record with jobs is so poor, my guess is he is not even working. I think I found the answer on the last day I was there, though. I was helping him clean up his place a little bit and went to put his shoes back in the closet when I noticed a whole bunch of women's shoes in there. When I asked my father whose shoes those were, he answered really quickly that they were his, as if he was totally unprepared to come up with a decent lie. So he has either gone down the road of cross dressing or he is there because of a woman."

"So has he spoken with you since you left? How did he end things?"

"No, he hasn't spoken to me since. As far as ending things, it was classic my father. Before I left he gave me 200 dollars and told me I should buy some lottery tickets, no joke. And the funniest thing is that after he told me to buy lottery tickets he said I owe him half if I win. Wow. This is a man who has never paid a dime of child support and doesn't even send me gifts for some of my birthdays."

"Hope,...*he paused as if to collect his thoughts and erase the half-surprised half-pensive look from his face*, before we go any further, do you mind if I react in a more human way to your stories and feelings about them? Most counselors are taught not to react to their patient's stories because they need to remain neutral, objective, and supposedly they have heard it all before. But I feel it is pretty disingenuous to respond in that manner, and the responsibility should be with the counselor to be human and remain objective at the same time. So if I say 'wow,' or 'that seems pretty crazy,' or I shake my head, or laugh a little when you are making light of your dark circumstances, it is only to try to be more human with you, react how you may react, and understand your feelings a little bit better. I have come to realize dealing with students is a whole new world because so many of them are so impressionable and fragile, but genuinely seeking out anyone who understands them, essentially 'gets' them. So if I acted like some neutral, stoic observer I think my relationship with you and them is already lost. Trust me, I was brought up to believe most problems are solved without using any emotion and so it has been a struggle for me to fight against that notion. My style of communication has definitely developed and I just wanted to be upfront with you, so hopefully you can come to trust me as authentic and genuine."

I was not sure how to react to what I just heard. In my world, I have never heard someone in a position of power and authority be so vulnerable and humble. It was as if he was speaking in a different language. I still wanted to hold back though…I know what adults have done to me in the past when I let my guard down. "Thank you for your words and for hearing my…stories. I want to say stories, but this is my life. I often wish these were just stories told by someone else and I could be a part of them in some surreal fashion, but this is my life."

Fall

Chapter 2: My Story

"Hope, I know in our first session we spent a little bit of time talking about what is currently going on in your life as well as your near distant past, *Mr. Morris said*. I appreciate you opening up to me. I know this might sound too psychoanalytic, but some of your family issues are probably from patterns which started a long time ago, most likely before you were even born. It might make it easier to understand where things stand in your life today if I know your family history. Would you mind telling me your family story?

"Do we have all day?" *I asked*.

"We have plenty of time, trust me."

"Ok, here goes..."

My parents immigrated to America from Korea in the 1970s when Korea was still a developing country and America was the land of opportunity. That's South Korea, by the way. I don't know how many times people have asked me if I am from North Korea, which has been a totalitarian state forever and doesn't allow its citizens out unless they escape. Both of my parents were well-educated in their homeland, having attended universities which are considered the Harvard and Yale of Korea. My father was the eldest son of a large, wealthy and prestigious family, and my mother was the youngest daughter of a large, somewhat well-to-do family. In old school Korean culture, the eldest son was treated like a king, allowed to reign over the rest of his siblings, whereas the youngest daughter was almost non-existent. So was the case with my parents, as my father was able to have almost anything he wanted, and my mother had to scrape just to get any attention or recognition.

After emerging from a relatively third world war-torn nation, Korea was slowly becoming a bright spot in East Asia. It wasn't completely lacking in opportunities, but maybe both of my parents wanted to get away from the shadows of their own families. My father's father was a well-educated doctor, teacher, author, and university president, whom my father could always daydream of being equal to, but could never live up to in reputation or prestige. And my mother was tired of having her feet held to the fire in her large family, literally. She still to this day tells the story about when she was a baby and her mother put her near the fire on a cold night to keep her warm. But apparently my grandmother forgot that my mother was there and the bottoms of her feet actually burned. She still has the scars today to prove it.

My mother had a nursing degree, and America was in short supply of nurses and doctors in the 1970s. My father had an architecture degree, which I can't imagine was an occupation in short supply. So I guess he hitched a ride on my mother's immigration plane and headed to America after they got married.

"And so is the tale of a struggling immigrant family in search of a better life in a new land."

We heard a deep man's voice with a British accent.

"The land so many yearned for was called America. And upon this—"

"Hey! Who are you and why are you talking about my story?" *I asked.*

"Well, I am the narrator. I am here to provide the lofty language and picturesque views people will appreciate."

"What, who said I needed you to help with my story? And why do you have a British accent, anyway?"

"I have a British accent because Americans think someone with a British accent is more intelligent and sophisticated, therefore it works well when telling an endearing and thought-provoking story about an immigrant girl coming to terms—"

"Hold it right there Mr. ClassyMcClasserson. So you are not even British, you just use a British accent to sound smarter?"

"Yes, I suppose," *he stated.*

"I would actually have to agree on that point, *Mr. Morris asserted*. I often wondered whether people would give me more respect and take me seriously if I had a British accent, a beard, and maybe a pocket watch connected by a gold chain to my three-piece suit, or maybe a monocle, I don't know."

"Oh brother. You guys should hang out then. So why do I need a fake British narrator again?" *I asked*.

"Well for one, you are a minor, *Narrator answered*. As this story is taking place in 1993, you are only 14 years old and minors are generally not great story tellers, if I may be so blunt. And second, I believe a story needs the type of deep and metaphoric language which is transcendental in nature, pulling people's minds to new heights."

"And why do I need deep and metaphoric language? I think my words will be well understood and I will be able to paint the picture of my life."

"Because people love complicated stories which are hard to understand but deep in meaning and purpose, *he expounded*. They love Thoreau, Hawthorne, and James Joyce."

"Wait a minute, *I countered*. I have done a lot of reading so far in my life, and I do know the authors and some of their works. I know Thoreau's *Walden* was very inspirational for many reasons, but he also seemed kinda kooky, spending exactly 2 years, 2 months, and 2 days living in a cabin in the woods by himself to gain some deep understanding. If he lived today would he love the Denny's *Grand Slam* breakfast because you get 2 pancakes, 2 eggs, 2 sausages, 2 bacon? And James Joyce, have you read all of his writing? He must've drank a lot or been high when he wrote, using meandering complicated patterns which are hard to follow. Have you ever tried to read *Ulysses*? It is like drunken stream of consciousness gibberish."

"Well, *Ulysses* is considered the best novel of all time according to many literary lists of the greatest novels," *he stated*.

"Really, I didn't see any of those lists."

"Well, some were published on the internet in the years 2005-2016."

"2016, what?!"

"Well, as a narrator I am not constrained by the year of your life and story. I can essentially time travel to gain pertinent information and oversight."

"Oh, ok. Thanks a lot. So I have a high-minded, fake British, time-travelling narrator who is helping me tell this story because I am too young?"

"If you choose to put it in those terms, I suppose," *he said.*

"Well, I think you are already ruining my story by jumping in the way you did and startling everyone. And now I am wasting valuable time arguing with you, so how about you take a back seat for a while and hopefully you won't pick the dumbest time to interrupt in the future."

"Agreed, um, except for the dumb part," *he said childishly.*

"Ok, I need to get back to my story then."

"Yes, please continue your story, Hope," *Mr. Morris said.*

I guess my parents didn't just jump on a plane and decide to come to America. A couple of my aunts from my mother's side were already here before them. My Aunt Cindy, (sorry but I am going to use her chosen American name, not her Korean and legal name. I know Cindy sounds like an odd choice for a Korean, but my parents, aunts, uncles, and cousins chose very generic American names which they thought would make them fit in). My Aunt Cindy was one of the oldest of my aunts and was a teenager a decade after the Korean War. She met an American soldier named

Charles when he was on R & R in Seoul during his service. Charlie was a Midwestern boy through and through and one of the nicest persons you could ever meet. He might be a 6 on the beauty scale, but his heart made him a 10 in my mind. So he met my aunt at a dance hall in Seoul where a lot of the soldiers hung out. She was working as a waitress, hostess, dishwasher, and saint. My grandparents always told her to be wary of the soldiers who came in, so she tried not to make too much eye contact, kept her distance, and always turned them down when they would ask her out. She knew almost no English, but had worked there long enough to know American pick-up lines, and probably even knew which ones were worse than others.

My uncle, somehow, was different than all the rest. The first time he noticed her he was standing on the side of the room as she moved from table to table picking up the empty dishes and pouring some more water and coffee. She noticed him too, but was quick to guard herself from pondering anything more. Throughout the night, he just calmly talked to other soldiers, stood there by himself, but always subtly checking in on her with his gaze. He even danced a few songs with some of the American nurses who were there that night, but even then he continued to seek her out with his eyes. She noticed him too, and even thought maybe she should give him a smile, although it scared her too much. As the night wore on and less dishes needed to be tended to, my aunt would stand at the side of the room as she waited for more people to finish at each table. It was then that my uncle made his move, but in a way my aunt came to adore. Instead of going up to her with some pick up line or silly joke, he just stood about 10 feet from her side, calmly and relaxed. He didn't say a word, but just shot a slight glance her way every once in a while without moving his head more than a few inches. After a few times, she reciprocated with a slight glance in his direction right about the time she saw his. After about 5 minutes of glancing back and forth, he lifted his eyebrow, shook his head so slightly, and gave her a tiny closed-mouth smile. She couldn't help herself and smiled back, almost giggling, and then looked down at the ground out of embarrassment. It seemed like this would continue to escalate until my aunt's manager signaled to her about a few tables that needed service. She almost skipped away to take care of her duties.

On the way back, she was carrying a load of dishes and cups and knew she would have to pass right by my uncle. As she got closer to him, she was unsure whether she should make complete eye contact, give a little smile, or keep her head down. As she pondered this moment she lost complete concentration on the items she was carrying and started to stumble ever so slightly.

My uncle, who hadn't taken his eyes off her burst into action and leapt over to her, placing his left hand flat under the dishes to prevent them from falling, and grabbing my aunt's left arm with his right hand to keep her from falling towards the ground. When she stood up straight, she smiled embarrassingly, and finally met him eye to eye. Well, actually not since she is tiny even by Korean standards and my uncle is average American height. So she gazed up at him as their eyes met. She stood there seemingly forever, waiting for him to say something. He just smiled. So she finally just said "thank you" in English. He said, "You're welcome," but nothing more. They stood there smiling for a couple more seconds, before she walked away to take the dishes and cups to the kitchen. To her amazement, though, by the time she returned to the hall he was nowhere to be seen. She was finally hoping for a line, even if it was a terrible one. But it didn't matter because he had already won her over without even saying a word.

My uncle was back a few days later and this time wasted no time finding my aunt and striking up a conversation. And strike up a conversation they did, in the weirdest way. My uncle knew pretty much no Korean words and my aunt knew next to no English words. It probably would have been the same if they just grunted subtly at each other while smiling and looking into each other's eyes. Even to this day my aunt's English is pretty bad and my uncle still only knows a couple of words in Korean. How they communicate is beyond me. I guess they are the best spokespeople for what a love language really is.

They later moved to America after getting married and both worked really hard at the factories throughout the Midwest, and owned small businesses on the side. They had children and developed a great future for many generations to come.

Narrator said, "How wonderful the love was between the brave soldier and native girl from a distant land with a different language and culture. So tells the story of two families from opposite ends of the earth melding into one, with hard work, love, peace, and harmony as the backbone of their lives together."

"Native girl? *I objected*. Um, she was pretty educated and just happened to speak a different language than English."

"I meant native as she was just 'native' to Korea."

"Well, in English, native can be interpreted as 'primitive' or at least closer to primitive if you don't reference the country in the same context. And why not choose to use the word 'native' to describe my uncle. He is native to America isn't he?"

"Because then he would be referred to as a 'Native American,' which has an entirely different meaning as I am sure you are aware. Is your uncle Native American?"

"No. Ugh. Don't you already know the answer? I thought you could see into the future and you know everything."

"I don't know everything, *he continued,* as I am restricted to the surrounding world, and do not know your entire story until you tell me. I cannot look at information surrounding your life until you reveal it. If you tell me your uncle's first and last name I can run a search to see if he is Native American, or whether he has been arrested, or if he owes money to people, or how much his house is worth—"

"Ok, ok. What? How much his house is worth? Is that within your narrator powers?"

"No, in the future everyone can know how much everyone else's house is worth."

"That doesn't seem like a very good thing to know."

"Oh, no, *he continued,* it is a very useful tool. In the future privacy is of no use to society. Knowing everything about family members and even strangers is important. It is also easy to spy on people without having to speak with them. It is common to become friends with people online so you never really have to see them in person. And you get to know so many details about them, such as your neighbor who really enjoys doing work for charity and helping those in need, or your other neighbor who takes tons of pictures with other women who are not his wife because he is one of those middle-aged cool guys. Very useful indeed."

"Ok, hopefully the future is not as creepy as you are making it sound. Also, I don't want to know about the future. I mean, as a native Chicagoan, next you are going to tell me that the Cubs won the World Series, like in the *Back to the Future* movie."

"Well, now that you mention it—"

"Ok, just stop. Please go back to wherever you hang out."

"I hang out everywhere. I have no boundaries."

"Clearly. Now shut it."

Back to my story of course, and another point you missed. Yes, my aunt and uncle have a wonderful love. It is the type of love I would only wish for. But it wasn't always that easy. Love and marriage is hard enough, but to have two different countries, languages, and cultures involved makes it even tougher. When my aunt and uncle came back to America after getting married, both families were not excited about their relationship. My younger aunts really liked my uncle because he was so nice to them and used to bring them American candy when he was visiting my aunt, which was a rarity in 1960s Korea. But my grandparents knew my uncle was not highly educated, and didn't exude the proper etiquette and class they were looking for in their daughter's husband. After returning, my uncle was able to secure a job at the Ford plant in Michigan and was later able to get my aunt a job there as well. Between the two of them they made decent money and were able to start a family. The crazy part was that my grandparents, still living in Korea, did not support my aunt and uncle's work because they thought it was too lower class, too blue collar. Two blue collar jobs in America would make someone rich in Korea, but somehow the class of a person in another country mattered to my family.

My Uncle Charlie appeared to let any criticism roll off his back, though, or maybe he wasn't even aware of it. Because Charlie and Cindy came from families who spoke different languages, they could act as the filter for any communication from their respective families. Who knows what they actually relayed to each other.

My uncle also helped many of my aunt's siblings immigrate to America, as well as land blue collar jobs once they got here. Eventually I think they came to appreciate my uncle's work on their behalf, but for some reason many of them still regarded those types of jobs as beneath them. And they didn't like the fact that people treated them a certain way based on their job status. They believed they were far more educated and sophisticated than the people they worked next to, but felt the language barrier was what held them back. I guess it would be difficult if people considered me less intelligent because of a language barrier or accent, even if I were educated and smart.

So my parents came over from Korea after they saw many relatives on my mother's side move here and at least survive. They settled in a northeast neighborhood of Chicago. It was right along the lake, prime real estate as they say, but no one wanted to live there at the time. And when I say no one, I actually mean middle class and professional white people. I remember being surrounded by every immigrant and racial group in my area.

"It is true that your neighborhood was heavily integrated in the late 1970s and early 1980s with Greeks, Russians, Native Americans, Vietnamese, Thai, and African Americans mostly, *Narrator explained*. It became almost a majority minority at one point. Public housing and Section 8 were prevalent throughout the area at that time. It was the most densely populated part of the city in the early 1980s, and residents were very concerned about new Section 8 and public housing developments."

"Thank you, Narrator, for finally adding something important to the story." As I was saying, I grew up in an area of Chicago which was heavily immigrant and heavily Section 8, which allowed us to fit right in, sort of. Even though my parents were married right out of college and they didn't have me until they were about 30 years old, you would think it would have allowed them to save up some money to provide for me and any future children, but that was far from the case. My mother worked as a nurse so my father could get his master's in architecture. Once he received his degree he was supposed to become the main breadwinner so they could start a family. One thing I can say about my father is that he is no breadwinner. My father is a dreamer, or more like daydreamer, rather than an optimist. I am not exactly sure how I would classify the difference except to say that an optimist understands hard work is required to achieve a dream, despite all of the struggles and failures. A dreamer, or daydreamer, seems to think the best successes in life will fall into his lap as long as he believes.

My father loved architecture as a craft and for its historical importance. And Chicago is a first-rate city when it comes to seeing some of the best buildings and structures in the world. Everyone from Burnham to Sullivan to Frank Lloyd Wright descended upon the city and surrounding areas during the late 1800s and early 1900s. I suppose the great Chicago Fire of 1871 allowed some of the best architectural minds of that era to eagerly come to the city and make their mark during the rebuilding. I can still remember my father showing me with excitement all of the intricate details of some of the famous and less famous buildings throughout the city. It was as if he was destined to be one of those major builders someday, leaving his mark which would stand the test of time.

Except he was my father. As I stated before, he was kind of a dreamer, with a huge dose of entitlement which came from his upbringing. At that time in Korea, there was so much classism and nepotism that people from upper class families were able to obtain good jobs relatively easily. For a Korean immigrant in America at that time, the only starting place was at the bottom, regardless of education or previous social status. So my father would have to start out as a draftsman and then work his way into an architect position, most likely working as a subordinate on a team, and then eventually branch out and supervise projects or open his own business. None of which seemed to suit my father in any measurable way. He didn't like the "hard work" aspect of the job.

Sure, he would love to design a ginormous building from scratch, with all the bells and whistles….some Corinthian columns here, some sculptures built into the façade here, maybe a unique style of window here, but to sit there and draft the specifics for someone else's small idea…maybe a 4,000 square foot building which would serve as a factory with a loading dock….that was like death to him. Not to mention my father's English still wasn't great, he was painfully shy, and was a bit of a socially awkward nerd, who didn't play well with others. I can still remember my mother speaking on his behalf when we went anywhere in public. He may whisper in her ear what he would like, but she was the one to go over and express our wishes to whomever she pleased. Even ordering food from McDonald's was difficult for him. So the workplace was probably like torture for my father. Having to speak to other people, get to know them, tell them about himself, how would he be able to do that? Or even for the work itself, which included communicating about the task at hand, or any changes which needed to be made. And you know what they say…the meager beaver doesn't get the worm, or the wood, and his dam floats away because it isn't strong enough, and his beaver children watch from the side of the river, crying, as their home floats away, or something like that. And then the beaver blames the trees, the forest, the other animals, and his beaver wife for his problems.

Narrator chimed in, "Hope, I do not believe you were using the proper words since I have never heard of that particular saying, and especially not in the context you used it. I am also pretty sure beavers cannot cry."

"Geez, Narrator, is there a program in your robotic mind which allows for humor, or irony, or embellishment? Like if I said, 'You are so annoying right now I want to kill you!' what would you think?"

"Well, I suppose I would not be afraid since you do not carry any weapons, are not very big, and humans cannot kill narrators anyway because we are technically in another parallel dimension. It is virtually impossible."

"Yes, please stay out of my dimension. Seriously, Narrator, please only speak up when you have something useful to add because you are getting kinda crazy."

As I was saying, I could see that my father's hopes hung on whether his work was so superior to others, which would make up for his lack of communication skills. Based on his track record, his work did not overcome that barrier. Maybe socializing and becoming friends would have been his saving grace. I can picture a situation where some of his co-workers want to go out for a drink, or watch a Bears or Cubs game together, or just go to the beach and play volleyball. My father would have preferred to do more "high-minded" things like go to the opera, or see the new exhibit at the Art Institute, or possibly check out another museum. I can imagine a co-worker stopping by his office on a Friday afternoon and asking my father to play volleyball at the beach, my father declining the invitation and instead asking him if he would like to go to the opera with him, his co-worker politely declining and then calling him a weirdo in his mind as he walked away. So as far as the team element which is necessary to develop in the workplace, I never saw any evidence of it. I don't ever remember seeing a co-worker come over to hang out or my father leaving home to do something with a friend. And my father never kept a job long enough to even develop any friendships.

The 3 of us lived in various 400 square foot studios throughout my time in Chicago. I am pretty sure we were living in Section 8 housing most of the time and also used food stamps, although that always caused tension in the home. My mother was a stay-at-home mom for most of the early years of my life. She could have gone back to work at any time since her services were in high demand and she was a hard worker. She was just about as opposite as you could get from my father. She was a scrapper, a comedian, brash and loud, would never take no for an answer. She would have no problem walking up to the President and demanding something if she thought it would help in a situation. As the youngest daughter of 11 children, she had to constantly fight for food, attention, admiration, and respect. She was confident at times, but deeply insecure at others, both resulting in an aggression about life and achievement. She was also really beautiful. I would classify her as a spunky beauty. So in the times of distress in my family, which was constant, my mother was picking up the pieces and making sure we had some kind of life. Every time my father was let go from another job, she offered to go back to work and make some money. He usually declined out of pride or because his dream-state did not allow himself to realize he was losing. They initially borrowed money from my grandmother on my father's side, often finding ways to sneak money to them without my grandfather knowing, lest he think of my father as a failure.

That money lasted a little while, but it was never enough to sustain us. And my parents' pride always caused them to spend money they didn't have when they were around friends or family. Whenever family members would visit us in Chicago, my parents always treated them to dinner as was a custom in Korea, or any culture I imagine. But my parents would always take them to a restaurant they could never afford and make up some reason why it was not a good time to have guests stay with them. The real answer was that guests wouldn't have even fit in our place, or been disappointed by the size and scrappiness. My parents always wanted it to appear as if we were doing well and my father was successful. My father would even offer to loan other family members money as a way to show how great he was doing, secretly hoping they would never say yes. The few times family members did say yes to his supposed generosity, my mother would always stop the transaction and blame herself by telling them she needed the money for some reason. It was crazy, then, when my father would often yell at her or hit her for doing such a thing to embarrass him. But I don't know where the money would've come from, unless he felt he could pass off Monopoly money to unsuspecting family members.

When the family money ran out, they turned to credit cards, which were not as plentiful back in the day. Sometimes they resorted to borrowing money from friends and family, often the very people they would brag to about doing so well. My father was always pontificating about how the next job was going to be so great and how someone would soon recognize his genius. He always thought he was better than the previous job he had, and often stated he was glad he had "quit" because the work was beneath him.

Meanwhile, my mother had been signing us up to receive Section 8 housing and food stamps without my father's knowledge. They had conversations about it many times before, which always resulted in a screaming match and some bruises for my mother. But she resisted his fury to get us some help financially, knowing we would otherwise be on the street. Pulling off the Section 8 was the hard part, as she had to convince my father to live in subsidized housing without him knowing about it. Some buildings had a few Section 8 residents, and some were entirely Section 8. My mother would often research a building nearby which accepted Section 8 and sign up for a unit. She often found a building where not everyone was subsidized, worried it would tip my father off if somehow a neighbor mentioned it. Then she would tell him that she was able to score a great deal on a new apartment. Whether my father was completely oblivious, or knew in the back of his mind we were receiving government aid but wouldn't say anything (which would allow him to keep his pride and the façade of a successful self-made man) we were not sure, but he went along with the plan. It didn't seem to make any difference in the scenery either, as we were usually moving from one 400 square foot crappy studio apartment to another 400 square foot crappy studio apartment.

The food plan was a little bit easier. My father was so bad with money that he wouldn't have known whether food came from Aldi or an expensive grocery store. So my mother applied for food stamps and would hide them in her purse. My father would give her money for groceries which would never have been enough to feed the family. I don't know if he expected her to barter with the grocery store, or for her to start a farm in the middle of the city and harvest food herself, but he was clearly in a dream-state when thinking such little money would sustain us. So my mother would do the shopping herself, supplementing with the food stamps. We would also go around the neighborhood and hit up all of the food pantries to get some free staples. Sometimes my mother would even take me for lunch at one of the homeless shelters before I started going to school.

As stated before, I first grew up in an area which was a melting pot of minorities, although I am not sure how much melting was going on. There were so many hard-working groups in the area who owned small businesses, including diners, restaurants, and dry cleaners. A few of our neighbors ran housecleaning services as well. Many people had various service sector and menial jobs throughout the city. I really didn't get to know many of our neighbors very well, as most people in these high rise apartment buildings kept to themselves, and my parents were no different. It seemed as if most other minority groups stuck to their own nationalities, ethnicities, and races, as was the case with my parents. We rarely hung out with anyone but Koreans, and since there were very few Koreans in the area, we didn't hang out with very many people.

It was a weird hierarchy of people. From my observations, it was always better to be an American-born white. No one seemed to give them a hard time in my neighborhood or school. Some of the Greeks or Eastern Europeans appeared to fit in as well, even though there were distinct cultural differences. The East Asians, including a few Chinese and Koreans, didn't fit in very easily. We had different looking faces and eyes, and distinctly different cultural patterns. There were also a few Southeast Asians, which included Vietnamese and Thai. It was probably because of our parents' generation, but a lot of the East Asians and Southeast Asians didn't hang out with each other. I now know based on conversations with my family members and other Koreans, many East Asians often viewed themselves in a higher class than Southeast Asians. That is too bad, because I could've used some friends in the neighborhood who looked more like me, even if our backgrounds were from different countries and cultures. The people I felt the worst for were the blacks, or African Americans as they are beginning to be referred to today. I am no cultural expert, but it appeared as if they were at the bottom of the minority hierarchy based on how people treated them, my family included. Many were hard-working and raising good families, but were still somehow thought of as being lower class than other minorities. I mean, in my neighborhood, someone could've been white and handing out Nazi propaganda material, Russian-American and espousing communism or Vietnamese and actually fought for the Viet Cong against us, and still been held in higher regard than the blacks. It was sad to see.

"Hope, I see no specific information regarding the hierarchy of minorities, as you describe. Are you sure this was accurate to your neighborhood?" *Narrator asked.*

"Oh, there was a hierarchy, just not written down. In Korea, determining hierarchy is so much easier because it is based on more of a class system in relation to family history, education, wealth, and occupation. In America, it is a little more subtle at times, but race, culture, education and money definitely have an influence. Narrator, you just have to read between the lines sometimes, and before you answer, it is simply a saying because we both know there are white spaces between the lines and can't actually be read."

"Noted. I wish the class system did not exist in any culture or country," *he said.*

"Oh, really, then how come you are what sounds like a British white male? Isn't that, from a historical perspective, one of the most class-obsessed societies, and drove your empire to go through the world conquering all kinds of other countries and cultures."

"I would not say we were conquering other societies, *he said*. They generally let us into their country or territory as we were exploring. We colonized their area and usually educated and civilized them. That does not sound so bad, does it?

"They weren't civil to each other?"

"They might have been civil to each other at times, but they weren't civilized," *he stated*.

"What does it mean to be civilized?"

"Well, of course, educated, follow certain rules in a society, uphold certain norms and truths, be well-spoken, properly mannered, and respectful of authority."

"Uh huh. So the British Empire was formed as a service to the rest of the world? Making sure these other wild and savage peoples were taught how to live proper lives?" *I asked sarcastically*.

"Correct. Look at all of the former colonies of Britain today, including America. So many countries have thrived long after the British Empire left its footprint on their societies. Try to name one country or territory worse off today because of the influence of Britain on its history."

"Oh, I don't know, how about the continent of Africa, and the slave trade which occurred throughout the world, mostly at the direction of the British initially," *I stated*.

"Well, although we can all agree slavery was a terrible idea, most of the British involved at the time were just following the rules of those African countries and tribes. When warring tribes fought a battle, the losing tribes were often subjected to slavery. The British were simply facilitating those rules at the time, and making a profit in the process."

"Oh, I see, *I objected*. What happened to the idea of civilizing others? Now they were just following the rules, rules which were totally uncivilized, harsh, and abominable. Why were the British merchants and colonists not educating these tribes about how uncivilized they were being and finding better rules for their society? I think it was because they were exploiting these areas, the same way they exploited other areas to gain access to valuable natural resources. They treated these other human beings as a natural resource, one which would become just like any other commodity, to be traded on the market. And look at the result of their actions. 130 years after the end of slavery in America, we as a society are still dealing with the idea of black people being treated like lesser human beings."

And it was no different in my family. I still remember my father giving me a lot of talks about avoiding black people, especially in social situations. We would go to the beach and my parents would often subtly find ways for me to stop playing with someone because he or she was black, which often left me with no one to play with. I was essentially taught from such an early age that I should avoid black people at all costs. I even remember, as a little girl, holding my breath when I was around them. I am not even sure why. Maybe I thought if we breathed the same air I would be harmed in some way. I blame my father mostly. His class obsession and sense of entitlement knew no bounds. Here we were, living in a slummy apartment, taking Section 8, living on food stamps, unable to speak the language very well, and yet we were so much better than these "lowly" black people. It makes me shiver when I think about it today. Especially because of all of the hurt and pain others caused me in the years to come, based on my race and cultural differences.

Sometimes I would ask my father why I shouldn't hang out with certain people and he would give me a long diatribe about how certain races and cultures are just better than others, and how our blood was very pure and over time our culture was able to ascend because of our dynasties in Korean history. Which makes almost no sense based upon the fact that Korea was subject to foreign occupation for most of the 20th century. The Americans were really the only force to stop all of the occupiers, which I am grateful to. And now my father was giving me so many talks about how we are better than all these other races, even the white Americans who helped free us from civil war and a definite future of poverty and isolation. I guess my father was just obsessed with high culture, which is why it was always the opera, or the symphony, or art and architecture which was so enlightening in his mind. It could also be why when I think about all of the extracurricular activities I did, they could definitely be categorized as high culture. I took piano lessons, tennis, golf, dance, and even horseback riding. Oh, but I forgot to mention that I took all of these expensive lessons after my parents divorced. My father would yell at my mother, tell her I should be in all of these high culture activities, but never paid a dime for any of them.

"Hope, thank you so much for sharing your story, *Mr. Morris said.* I know a lot of those memories are painful, especially the ones regarding the hardships you endured as a child. Based on your history, it seems as if your parents' views about classism drove them to make some bad choices, especially in the case of your father. Do you feel as if you have been influenced by them regarding class or social stature?"

"I dunno, *I said.* I don't really look at people that way so I hope I see people for who they are instead of what class they are in. And for me, I have seen what it is like to live in the lower class and barely get by. Hopefully I have gained some sort of perspective and it helps me treat others better because I know what it is like to struggle to fit in and have so little in this world. I understand that my parents came from a culture and country which really valued class, but America is so much different for immigrants and they needed to just figure out how to get by. Mostly, I think my father didn't shed his old ways and my mother went along with it I guess. I know they probably struggled to fit in and maybe it was really hard for them to adapt. For me, I totally understand that, because each new school means having to fit in again and it is really hard, and I have been to so many different schools already in my life. And not being like everyone else is difficult too, especially if you look different. Maybe I have a head start on my parents, though, because although I look different, I was at least born in this country and understand its ways a little bit. I think my mother is adaptable, but I don't think my father will ever truly adapt. And all of his failures fell on my mother and me."

"I feel bad that you grew up in an area where you didn't really fit in, as well as the hardship of trying to adapt to new locations. How has that affected your life so far?" *he asked*.

"I definitely don't feel comfortable around people who are different than me, but not because of their differences. I always think they are going to look at me and see the differences between us right away. I have always been in the minority when it comes to my race and it is hard to have that comfortable feeling of knowing I am like everyone else. I just expect to be an outsider at first, but hopefully over time people look at me as just one of them, one of the group."

"Do you think you fit in at this school?" *he asked*.

"No, I don't yet. Although I have become used to new schools so I know there is a process. Sometimes I don't try very hard to meet new friends because I know they will be out of my life if we move somewhere new. Hopefully we will be here for a while so I can actually have some lasting friendships, but I dunno. I try not to think about it too much because it will just bum me out."

Fall

Chapter 3: They're all White, but that's Alright

I have been feeling pretty good since my first few sessions with Mr. Morris. I have never known someone who has taken the time to sit down with me and actually listen to my issues, my life. I know it's his job, but he seems genuinely interested in what I am about. Not like my father, or my mother for that matter. She will listen to me, but I believe she thinks I am weak and I should just learn to forget about things. Obviously, I am not like that, and I know I tend to overthink everything, but pondering is what I do as an only child. I have gotten so used to being in my own head that there is a genuine comfort when I am just letting my thoughts drift off and see where they take me. Of course, there are some dark thoughts which hurt me, so maybe I will have to become a poet someday, or a painter, or maybe an artist. Artists like to dwell on aspects of their own lives, or live with a brooding demeanor. It is almost as if you can't be an artist if you are a really happy person.

On a more normal note I guess, I met a couple of new friends. It took me a little while because I tend to be shy when I first meet others, especially in new schools, but I hope I will be friends with these girls for a long time. They are total opposites, which is kinda cool. I think I am somewhere in the middle, so I can see aspects of myself in each person.

Stacy and Kelly are their names. I know, why do so many American names end in a "y" or "ie"? Maybe it provides a certain amount of pep to the name. Maybe someday someone will call me Hopey, so I can be just like these other girls. Anyway, over the last few months we have become almost inseparable in school and out. Kelly is pretty down to earth and laid back. She has long blonde hair and I would say on the medium-build side. I'm not saying she is fat, cause she is definitely not, but she is not really skinny either. I guess she is just average size. Stacy is on the tennis team with me and you can tell she is really athletic. She is kinda tall, with brown hair, and in really good shape. I wish I were in as good a shape as she is, but I don't think it's possible. I am thin, but have that whole Asian body going on. We are thin and have a little bit of shape, but mostly not a lot of curves on either end. Stacy, on the other hand, actually has some muscle and curves from her years of sports, or maybe it is just natural, I dunno. It makes Stacy popular with the guys, though. Whenever we are all together, I always notice guys checking her out. And she is aware of it as well, and is usually kind of a flirt. I don't know how she learned how to act around guys, but she has a gift for attracting them. The way she talks, stands, it all has this natural element I clearly do not possess. Even when she says "hi" to boys it is different than I am used to. It is almost as if she is inviting them to some happy place by just saying "hi" in a flirty way. And the way she stands appears to send out signals. I don't think I could ever copy it, but she generally stands at some sort of angle which accentuates her body, especially her butt. It is almost as if she is prompting guys to have a laser gaze right on her behind. She never just stands straight up and talks to them. When the guys are close she always has one leg out a little bit, bent, and one hand on her hip, her butt thrust to the side a little. When we are at our lockers she is turned toward me at an angle, I guess so she can let her rear face out to any onlookers. I wish I had her confidence. I wonder what would happen if I were around a lot of other Koreans and they noticed I was trying to accentuate my body. They would probably tell their parents, who would tell my mother, and my mother would say I was acting inappropriate. But then I would wonder how my mother attracts all of these Korean dudes. Maybe she puts her behind out there for them to notice, I dunno.

Kelly doesn't have the magic touch with guys, kinda like me. We both get really shy when guys are around and don't know what to say. Kelly has a really cute face, but I think she is a little bit insecure about her body. High school is like a competition and I know she feels as if she isn't skinny enough. I, on the other hand, am not worried about my body since I am skinny, but sometimes I think about my face. I know I can be cute to some guys, but I am not sure if they like Korean faces or think I look weird. At least I have some cool clothes now that my mother has some money, and she allows me to go and get my own haircut. I am not always sure what is in-style in terms of hair, so I just ask the hairdresser to give me something which looks cool. I don't always know if they are good at cutting Asian hair though. It is thicker and straight, and can go horribly wrong if the person never cuts Asian hair. At least with my hair, it is pretty long, so I can hide any mistakes. But I have seen Korean guys where it looks as if someone hacked their hair up with an ax, because it is so uneven or it just sticks out in all the wrong places. At least I am beyond the bowl cut years, though. I don't know what it is about Asian kids and bowl cuts, but it is really annoying.

I had a bowl cut until I was about 8 or 9 years old. I think it was to save money, so my parents or a friend would cut my hair. I don't remember them ever using an actual bowl, but it certainly looked that way. And I got glasses at a young age too. Nothing like going to school with glasses and a bowl cut.

So now I am entering into the awkward girl/woman years. I am not sure what to do. Kelly and I try to talk to guys when they come around, but I'm not sure whether I should make jokes or say something profound, or interesting. Kelly is too shy to help, and I could never be able to pull off what Stacy does. I don't understand small talk either. Maybe because my parents didn't socialize much, or maybe it is an American thing, but small talk to me is really hard. I guess it is a way to start off a conversation, get comfortable, and then talk about something more interesting once the ice is broken. With Stacy, it seems so natural. Kind of like, "Hey, saw you in class. Really boring, right, and then Mr. Gray was going on and on about who knows what. Hey, want to maybe grab a shake after practice tonight. If my parents aren't home until later, maybe you could come over and make out with me? Oh, cool, then, sounds like a plan." Ok, it isn't exactly that simple, but it's almost as if that is what the guys hear when she is talking to them. I would get nervous and probably say something like, "Hey, I like your pants. I mean, no. I just came from class. Do you like sandwiches? I ate one for lunch. Uh....ok gotta go, bye." Or if it were Kelly and me together, we would just stand there and not say a word, and probably stare.

Kelly and her family are really down to earth. Her father works for one of the American automakers and her mother is a stay-at-home mom since she has a couple of younger siblings. Whenever I am over at their house I feel at ease. Her mother is really sweet and her father is like a big, jovial teddy bear. They don't have too many rules to follow and everyone in the family gets along. Her parents really pay attention to all of the kids, always asking them how their days went, what they think about this and that, even involving them in decision-making about dinner, what to do on the weekends, or even vacations. It is so eye-opening to see parents and kids who are not on such separate levels. With my parents, and so many other Korean parents, it is such a top down model where the kids are spoken to, instead of spoken with. I would never consider just blurting out my opinion about anything in front of my father, unless he specifically asked me to do so, which never happened. I can state my opinion with my mother now, but mostly because she accepts that about American lifestyle, or because it is the only way I can really get through to her. My mother is usually in her own-world kind of mode, and I almost have to yell at her to get her to notice me or do something for me. That is one aspect I love about American culture. Stating your opinion is looked upon as a showcase of intelligence or independence. I have so many opinions I wish I could have told my parents, especially when they were acting crazy.

Also, Kelly's family allows for the free flow of opinions, but people don't appear to get very upset with each other based on what was said. It must be because they all have a good sense of humor. It is almost expected that everyone pokes fun at each other. I think it is a way of letting off steam. I saw Kelly's parents get into minor arguments at times, and it appeared that either her father or mother would throw in a few sarcastic comments to take the edge off the dispute and help resolve the conflict. Almost as if the conflict became a bit of a joke to them. I never experienced that growing up. My parents, and with my mother's other relationships for that matter, produced harshness or rage by the end of the argument. Nothing was able to take the edge off of those conversations. And any dose of humor would have been seen as disrespectful or making light of the situation, rather than turning the situation on its head and laughing about it.

Kelly's parents also have hobbies, which is something I didn't see in my family. Some of my older relatives, who own dry cleaners, seem to have two modes…work and sleep. When they aren't working at work, they are working at home, then they sleep. I guess the idea is that everything they do, they do for their children, and hobbies don't help their children at all. My parents do value the idea of work, although my mother is the only one I have seen working really hard. I guess my father likes the arts and museums, but I wouldn't say it is a hobby. So between my parents, aunts, and uncles, I haven't seen anyone with a real hobby. So it is kinda cool to see parents with some hobbies. Kelly's mother likes to knit. Whenever we are sitting around she has her knitting needles out and spool of yarn next to her. She loves to make hats, baby blankets, and even bed-sized blankets. She is so good that she could make just about any pattern. And because their family is made up of big sports fans, she knits a whole bunch of University of Michigan, Detroit Lions, or Detroit Tigers themed items. It is pretty cool to see. It is also cool because even though the goal is to produce this elaborate piece of fabric at the end, I think she knits because she really enjoys it as she is doing it. It doesn't relate to some grand solution which benefits her or the family in any substantial manner. I guess that is what a hobby is supposed to be. You actually enjoy doing something in the moment. I can't see my parents ever getting that concept, or some of my other relatives, for that matter. They work to provide for their families, or work to become rich and move up in the class order. They want their kids to have better lives than them. I totally understand. Because who would really, truly enjoy some of the jobs they have. Working at the dry cleaners is tough work, toiling in sweltering conditions for 15 hours a day sometimes, 6 or 7 days a week. Or working at factories, double shifts when available. No one ever said, "When I get some free time I am going to press shirts all day or put the same part into the same engine for 10 hours straight."

But some of my friends' parents do have these types of jobs too, and some of them do have hobbies. Maybe they have extra time because they aren't obsessed with their kids' educations the way my parents were, or so many other Korean parents are. Regardless, I am able to see parents who appreciate something outside of working or raising children. For Kelly's father, he really likes boats. My guess is that they don't have a lot of money, but I suppose they saved up so they could buy a pretty good sized boat. They like to take it out to Lake Michigan, or some other local lakes any chance they get. I really hope I get a chance to go out on their boat since I really love being on the water. I remember sailing on a boat with my cousin and a friend about a year or so ago. We just cruised around Lake Michigan on a Saturday afternoon while my cousin fished and we all hung out. We basked in the sun, listened to music, and laughed a lot. That night we slept below deck. I remember waking up during the night, so I decided to go up to the main deck. It was so peaceful to sit there and look up at the stars and moon. I decided at that moment I really loved being on the water. Looking off into the distance was so calming to me for some reason. It was as if the distance represented the future, a goal perhaps, or just a way to discover something new. There were no limitations to what I saw beyond the horizon.

Stacy has a fiery personality I was immediately drawn to. We met at fall tennis club. I was surprised to meet her and become friends with her quickly because I figured she would already have a lot of friends, as she seemed like the popular type. But like me, she is from a divorced family and her mother had just moved here from a rougher area around Detroit. She doesn't see her father that much either, but at least he is in the picture. I think we bonded because we are from a similar situation. And she actually thought I was cool because I was different. She told me a few times I was the only Asian friend she had ever had and really liked being around me because of our different cultures. Stacy always wants me to teach her swear words in Korean so she can use them when she is really mad at other people, and thinks it is cool to know what she is calling them even if they don't.

The way she talks is really interesting to me too. She appears to just say whatever she wants to whomever she wants to. Coming from such a guarded environment where what was said in public had to be so proper or respectful, her speech is like a breath of fresh air. It also helps me laugh about my own situation because of the way she talks about hers. She has no problem calling her dad a bum if he failed to visit her on the weekend as he promised to, or if he hadn't talked to her in a while. Sometimes she calls the guys her mom dates losers. When I asked her about her mom's newest boyfriend one time she responded, "Oh yeah, you mean the latest loser?" It is freeing to see that it is normal to laugh about these kind of tragic events in the life of a teenager. I struggle between my Korean upbringing of manners, respect, and keeping things to myself when talking to outsiders, and this American style Stacy and some others seem to exhibit. I would generally never tell an outsider about the dirty laundry in my family because of the shame it would bring my mother and father, and I guess me as well. Maybe if we were living in a small town environment, most Americans would keep things to themselves too, for fear reputations could be tarnished. The Korean community always appeared small, no matter where we lived. So appearance and reputation mattered so much. In larger white communities, I guess most people didn't think their reputations could be as tarnished because word didn't get around as fast. The community was more fractured, heterogeneous. One family's problem was just a small part of the larger community. It wasn't enough to really make a difference. Whereas the small, homogenous Korean community notices anything out of the ordinary. Although I think this was originally a Japanese saying, my parents used to tell me in Korean all the time, "The nail that sticks out gets hammered down."

Because Stacy was so comfortable talking about her family's issues, I slowly became willing to share things with her. It was interesting because she doesn't mince words and wants to boil everything I say down to a simple truth. In her search for the nitty gritty, she takes away all of the noise, justification, moral relativism, and tells it like it is. I really appreciate it. She often responds to my comments, "Your father should talk to you more or he is a bum…Your mother has problems…She should pay attention to you…Your mother works too much…She should take a chill pill…Sounds like your mom likes losers just like my mom." It was so cool because I often made up these really complicated arguments in my head as to why my parents did the things they did. Some of it was based on their upbringing, or culture, or their immigrant status, or the hope they were in transition and close to becoming better people.

Regardless of the specific argument, it always ended up with me justifying their behavior and often even blaming myself. I thought if I were a better daughter, more accomplished, and what they wanted me to be in life, then they would pay attention to me more and love me more. Maybe if I were on track to becoming a doctor my father would really take an interest in my life. Maybe if there was something about me my mother could brag to her friends about, then she would be really close to me and encourage me.

Even if Stacy sticks out, as the Korean saying goes, she isn't a nail, she is a hammer. She talks back to her parents when they are in the wrong, which is frequent. She gets to know other girls and takes charge of social situations right away. Boys are drawn to her and it is as if she is making them wait in line to get to know her, but not in some princessy sort of way. The cool part about her is she does what she wants, and lets everyone else try to figure her out. I am so much the opposite. I try to figure everyone else out in an attempt to fit in and won't act until I know I am doing the "right" thing from a social or cultural perspective. Stacy is quick thinking and natural in social situations, so I actually think she is doing the "right" or most popular thing. Maybe she is making the rules, and the rule-maker is always right.

Fall

Chapter 4: Well Gook You Too

"In the last few sessions we have discussed your adjustment to this new school, *Mr. Morris stated.* The fact that you met some friends and are starting to enjoy your classes indicates in my mind that the process is starting to go a little more smoothly. What was it like when you joined other new schools or moved to new locations with your mother?"

There is no simple answer to that question. Growing up in an area with few Koreans, or even Asians was difficult. I heard all of the stereotypes about Asians being good in school, good at math, our food smelling funny, our hair looking different, and especially our different shaped eyes. When we moved away from our more immigrant-heavy area and into an area which was mostly white, things changed quite a bit for me. Instead of being one of many "different" kids, I became "the" different kid. I went to a junior high which was almost all white. The area had a lot of second and third generation Polish Americans. A lot of the fathers tended to be cops, firefighters, work in construction or own small businesses. It sounded like a lot of hard-working people who were trying to get ahead, and had been the subject of jokes and comments as well. I had been in Chicago long enough to hear a lot of Pollock jokes, and most of them portrayed the Polish as dumb and ignorant. So it was pretty surprising that many of the kids at my school made fun of me because of how I looked or my family talked, at least initially. I would have thought they would be more sympathetic, especially if they had experienced cruel jokes or comments directed at them because of their heritage. Maybe that is how it worked, though. Each group thinks they are better or more normal than another, and white, second generation, Polish American kids were higher up on the scale than a second generation Korean American kid.

I still remember other students asking me what I was, as in just, "What are you?" That was always funny because I knew what they meant, but it was a ridiculous question to ask an actual human being. Sometimes just to play with them I would say, "I'm an American," or maybe, "I am a human just like you," cause I figured they didn't think I was an alien. Sometimes they would continue to ask and I would eventually tell them I was Korean. Some kids even said, "What's a Korean?" That was funny too. "Well, a Korean is a human from the distant land of Korea," I remember saying on occasion. Some kids would presume to know about me already, or maybe thought they were going to get bonus points by asking upon meeting me, "Are you Chinese or Japanese?" I would usually answer "neither," sometimes without providing them any additional info unless they asked, which would throw them for a loop because they ran out of ideas at that point. I could see the wheels turning in their heads as they searched for any bit of information which could make them understand how I could be Asian, but not Chinese or Japanese.

There were kids on the playground who would sing, basically directly to me, the whole "Chinese, Japanese, dirty knees, look at these" song. A few kids had a different version which went, "Chinese, Japanese, dirty knees, money please." Sometimes I would ignore it or sometimes I would point out that I am not Chinese or Japanese so the song meant nothing to me. Occasionally I would ask if they knew what the song meant. Generally that resulted in blank stares and shrugged shoulders. To this day I am not sure of the exact meaning, but it definitely has something to do with subservient Asian women, possibly with a sexual aspect to it. Some kids actually argued the song was educational because it taught them which way different Asian eyes were slanted (during the song kids usually pull the corners of their eyes up or down when they are saying the words "Chinese" or "Japanese"). Even I knew it sounded ridiculous when they told me that.

"I am sorry they treated you this way based on the fact that you looked different than them, *Mr. Morris said*. Kids can be cruel. It is hard enough just being a kid with minor differences than others, but I imagine it is much tougher when the differences are larger and you are in the extreme minority."

Yeah, for sure. I still remember a day when I was in 7th grade and walking home from school by myself. A car slowed down and pulled up near me. The windows were rolled down and some teenage boy leaned out of the car and just yelled "chink" about as loud as he could. Everyone in the car laughed and then they just sped away. I remember starting to cry, not necessarily because his actual insult was so hurtful. It wasn't even the right racist word, if there is such a thing. It was more so because he and his friends took so much effort to say something hurtful. They went out of their way to single me out as a stranger in their town. Up until that point, I could handle a lot of the questions at school which might have been ignorant, the weird glances I would receive because of my food or if they saw me talk to my mother in Korean. Most of those times were probably a mix of curiosity with a fear of the unknown. I would probably offend many black students if I were in their presence as well. I may ask about their hair or whether they get sunburns, or other questions I thought were interesting but they thought were annoying or hurtful in some way. But this incident was purposeful and planned. It made me feel small and made me feel alone.

And it didn't make it any better when my mother got home and I explained the incident to her. She wasn't outright dismissive, as she stated that those people just didn't know any better and sometimes it is hard when we are the minority in certain areas. But it seemed to roll right off of her and she really didn't understand why it had hurt me so much. To her, if someone said something offensive or mean, she went right back at them with a comment. Or she just worked harder in order to prove those people wrong. She could drive a nicer car or believe she was smarter than them. Whatever she told herself in her head worked, because it appeared as if those types of incidents didn't enter her world. Maybe as an adult, she was so used to negative stereotypes that she developed a thick skin, or maybe her headstrong nature would just not allow any negative thoughts to get in.

This was the first time in a long time I wished my father was near. Although he didn't seem to have any solutions in life, I know he could feel what it was like to get kicked around. He knew what it was like to take abuse from the world and not have any way to retaliate. Sometimes when I was away from my father I understood him a little bit better. He probably felt abused by the world and wanted to stand up for himself. He was unable to do it, but the desire did not die out. So instead of standing up for himself in the world, he took all of that inner anger and placed it right on my mother and me. He ended up taking some shots, but he hit the wrong targets.

As I said before, the word chink wasn't even the right racist stereotype word to use. Chink was common for the Chinese, jap for the Japanese, and Koreans, well there wasn't always enough of us in America to get assigned a particular word. Sometimes people used the word gook for any Asian of any country, and if they used it for a Korean, in a weird way they would be accurate to its origination. Supposedly there are many gook-like sounding words which have been used to refer to Asians of various ethnicities in the past, but gook really became a popular word during the Korean War. The word guk in Korean means country. The word han originates from the Han Dynasty in Korean history. So hanguk would mean Korea using the Korean language. The word miguk (sounds like me gook) would be the word for America. So during World War II and the Korean War a lot of the soldiers might have interpreted Koreans saying or yelling "miguk" to the American soldiers as "Me gook," almost referring to themselves as gooks. It is pretty sad to think that Koreans were probably yelling out "miguk" to the soldiers because they were supporting the troops and wanted to show their gratitude toward America, and later the word gook was used as a put-down or racist word to Korean children living in America.

Narrator chimed in, "I must also point out that the term gook was widely used by Americans in the Vietnam War to describe the Vietnamese and there is also a word in Viatnamese which sounds similar to gook. Meiguo is a Vietnamese word, taken from its Chinese origin, which means America. It also sounds similar to 'Me gook' when interpreted by English speakers."

"Thank you, Narrator, *I said*. I empathize with the Vietnamese children out there who are subjected to the word gook as well. I am sure in addition to being seen as different in America, they may have been subjected to even more ridicule because of America's resentment towards the Vietnam War."

"I am sorry your mother wasn't as empathetic as she should have been, *Mr. Morris said*. Hopefully it is because she got used to those types of comments. It could be, however, that she only experienced those types of ignorant or racist comments as an adult, because she didn't move here until she was much older. It is different to experience malicious and callous words and actions as a child as opposed to an adult. Maybe she was unable to understand how much it hurt you."

"I hope so. I wonder how I would feel and what I would do if I heard those words as much today."

Narrator said, "If you would like, if someone calls you chink at your new school, I will tell him that it is an incorrect use of the word, and the correct word to use is gook."

"That is not the 'correct' word," *I blurted out*.

"Well, it is the correct word for the situation, as you pointed out."

"That is not what I am saying. I am pointing out the fact that even in their racism they are ignorant because they don't even know the right racist word to use. Not that there is ever a 'right' racist word."

"I see. They are extra racist."

"No, they are extra ignorant, *I stated*. And there is no correct use of that word. They shouldn't use any words like that. It is hurtful to me and all Asians to use any of those words. How about calling us by our names, or if you really like us, calling us friend, or girl, or dude, or any other positive slang word for friend."

"Ok, you two, *Mr. Morris interrupted*. I wish you had someone to empathize with or commiserate with during those times in your life. I know from any hurtful times in my life that it is always better to have siblings, friends, or parents to help you get through those tough times. Even if they just listened, I am sure it would have had a positive impact on the situation. Hopefully you will be able to find some friends at this school or in your new neighborhood who are able to empathize with you when you have tough times."

Fall

Chapter 5: Me and the TV

The last couple of sessions have been pretty laid back. I think Mr. Morris wanted to give me a break from some of the more serious conversations.

"Hope, I know we were just shooting the breeze the last couple of weeks to get to know each other better. I am hopeful it helps you trust me when we do get into more serious topics." *Mr. Morris looked pensive and a little apprehensive.*

"Sounds like a serious topic is coming our way, right? *I said sarcastically.*

"Very perceptive. Sorry for the lead up. I should have just asked. I know based on a few of the comments you made when telling your story a few weeks ago that your family has a history of domestic violence. Did your father ever strike you?"

"No, he just hit my mother, unless you include actual spanking."

"Why do you think that is?" *he asked.*

I don't know. I would love to think it is because I was his baby girl, his princess, but that is so far from the truth it is not even funny. My father always wanted a boy and I think he resented me at times because I wasn't one. He was never warm to me, but I don't think he thought I was ever a threat to him or his views, so maybe that is why he never hit me. My father was such a meager individual in all aspects of life. He lived in his head, in a world dominated by the intelligent, cultured, and elite. I think he believed he fell into that group based on this family name, upbringing, and education. The real world didn't seem to agree with his self-assessment. Maybe if he stayed in Korea it would have been different. Here in America, he was just another immigrant trying to get by and develop a life for himself and his family. He wasn't aggressive enough to go after a better opportunity, his poor English made him look stupid even though he was really smart, and his lack of adaptation left him with less choices. I think his personality just didn't fit with the hunger necessary to really thrive as an immigrant. He was too cerebral and living in the world of what "should be" instead of what "is." Over time he became more and more angry that the world would not bend or succumb to his inner world view. He was never one to be self-reflective enough to tell himself he needed to change, only that the world was wrong and it needed to change because his was the right way.

And my mother probably didn't help the situation either. She was so headstrong and aggressive in life. If something didn't bend to her will, she would go and try to bend it as much as possible until she was satisfied. She became the spokesperson for our family, and thus would speak on behalf of my father whenever something went wrong or something needed to get done. And sometimes the something needing to get done was related to my father himself. She would encourage him and push him to do better, to find a different job when he was let go from his previous one, and to speak up when something didn't go his way. As he became more inward with his thinking and behavior, she became more outward because the family needed that for balance. But as this happened, tension grew and their separation grew more apparent.

My father never developed any coping skills, how to let off steam. My mother doesn't really have any gentleness to her, so she never had the soft touch or word to calm him down. So I think as my father's anger turned inward, he blamed everything and everyone for his failures, which included my mother. He started turning his anger on her as all of this rage built inside him. I often think of it as a tea kettle which has something stuck in the spout. The steam has nowhere to go and it eventually explodes. He would hit her during an argument at first, mostly when they couldn't resolve anything verbally. Then he started hitting her over little things and more frequently. Sometimes he would come home with an angry thought or disagreement in his head and appeared ready to explode.

He became more violent and the end of their relationship occurred when my mother started sticking up for herself or fighting back. There were times where I even tried to get in the middle to protect my mother, but was usually pushed away pretty easily. My father wasn't much of a physical specimen, and you would never think of him as imposing, but my mother, as feisty as she was, was no match for him being barely over 5 feet tall and not much more than 100 lbs.

"In the end they received a divorce, right? Can you remember what finally prompted it?" *he asked.*

The last fight. I was eight years old at the time. It is burned in my memory, probably until the day I die. I am not sure exactly what prompted it. It is funny, when you spend time in an abusive situation you think you will remember every time it happened and just what triggered the latest burst of anger and abuse. I guess it is a defense mechanism you learn, thinking that somehow if you act a certain way and avoid certain topics, you can prevent any future episodes because you know all the triggers. But after a while you come to realize that the anger of the abuser has no logic, no specific trigger. The same sandwich can be made exactly the same way on two different days, but only one day do you get hit for making the sandwich incorrectly. So my parents on that day probably argued about the same non-garden-variety garden-variety topic as they had so many times before. My father was complaining about someone else for some reason. He started a rant about these "other people" in the world who were making everything so bad and somehow hurting him, the way he always seemed to lay blame. My mother must have made some contrary point or was just not interested in hearing his complaints, which set my father off. He turned his wrath on her, yelling that she wasn't on his side and didn't even try to understand. He started coming toward her until they were almost eye to eye, which meant my father had to tilt his head down a little bit. He almost screamed at my mother, "Why don't you get it?" or at least that is the closest English translation. My mother tried to stand up as tall as she could and essentially said back, "You're right, I don't get it. I don't know why you can't keep a job or support us, you can't get better at anything, or just be a man." I could see my father seething from the inside, almost about to boil over, his eyes were as wide and piercing as I have ever seen them, and he yelled out, "You don't respect me at all, do you?" My mother, drew her face even closer, straightened and tightened her shoulders, and defiantly stated without yelling and in a calm tone, "How could I respect you?"

Whatever pent up rage my father had boiling at the surface came exploding out at this very moment. He completely lost control and grabbed both of my mother's hands with one of his hands and then slapped her so hard across her head with the other. She lost her balance a little bit but did not fall down. As she was turned to the side just a little bit he took his hands and pushed her until her shoulder hit the wall. He hit her again like a boxer who had never learned how to connect a punch, just swinging wildly. Then my father grabbed my mother by the shoulders and threw her down to the ground. As she lied there on the ground he took his foot and pushed it against her neck and was using what looked like all of his force. My mother was able to push his foot away for an instant and turned over to get up. He took his foot and pressed it against her upper back, right under her neck. His face was all red and he had a look of rage in his eyes. He kept pressing his foot harder and harder while my mother was groaning and trying her hardest to move. Just then she shrieked in pain. I thought my father was going to kill her so I ran over and pleaded with him to stop. He just kept the pressure on and his face did not change at all. I moved closer to my mother's head and looked right at him and cried out for him to stop. As he looked at me I could see his face changing in almost an instant, as if he was embarrassed and didn't know what was going on. He looked down at his foot as if in amazement and I could see the pressure was beginning to be released as his body started to relax. He took a couple of deep breaths as if he had just run a marathon. His face was sweaty and his glasses were a little bit fogged up. So he took his glasses off and calmly wiped them off on his shirt.

My mother was still writhing in pain and screaming that there was something wrong with her. She told me to call my aunt right away because she couldn't get up. I looked over at the phone, and then looked at my father to see what I was supposed to do. He had a blank stare on his face, but seemed to indicate he was not going to fight my mother's request. I calmly walked to the phone and called my aunt. It is weird because even in that moment I was still trying to respect my parents' privacy and save them some embarrassment because I didn't tell my aunt any details. I just told her my mother would like her to come over, as my mother yelled from the ground that my aunt should come over because it was serious and she needed help.

After hanging up, my mother, in a tired and desperate tone, said she was going to call the police. She had threatened my father many times before regarding the police, but had never called them because he always convinced her that somehow she would get into trouble or she would bring shame to the family because so many people would find out about it. I could see this time was different and my father felt it too. So he told me to put my shoes on and that we were leaving. I said, "What about mother?" but he didn't respond. He just told me more adamantly to grab my shoes and that we had to leave.

We left the apartment, walking pretty fast down the sidewalk. My father was holding my hand and almost pulling me along, although we appeared to be going in no particular direction. It looked as if he was trying to find any place where we could hang out, or escape the police. He kept looking over his shoulder as if the cops were right on his tail or something. We kept walking by store after store, coffee shops, and restaurants. My father would sort of glance in to see if it was a suitable location, but none of them appeared sufficient.

So we finally got to a movie theater and for whatever reason we went right in. I was not sure why my father chose a movie theater. Did he think we were just out to see a Saturday matinee, or that the movie theater was dark so cops couldn't find us? I don't know what was going through his brain. He looked up at the movie selections and realized there was only one movie playing around this time. So he walked up to the girl behind the ticket booth and asked for 2 tickets to *Die Hard*. The girl, who was probably in high school, gave my father a surprised glare and then glanced at me, and then back at him. She took the money and gave us our tickets. At that point my father seemed to relax a bit and started to act as if we were just going to a movie and this day was no different than any other. He asked me if I wanted candy or popcorn, which is not something he would have ever done before. I was so torn at this point because I knew something was really wrong and I was worried about my mother, but I couldn't get up the nerve to ask my father about her. So I just politely said I would like some candy.

To this day I don't remember really seeing the movie. It was *Die Hard*. I was eight. There was lots of guns and violence. I remember the violence because it looked like the world I just came from, but I really didn't know how to process anything which was happening that day. I just sat there and blankly stared at the screen. The entire time I tried not to look at my father, although I occasionally glanced at him out of the corner of my eye. He had virtually no expression the entire time so I wasn't sure if he was upset, scared, sad, regretful, anything. After the movie we strolled out of the theater as if it was just a day in the park and we could saunter home. I wanted to walk faster to make sure my mother was alright, but my father was walking slowly and methodically, as if he was thinking about the situation and whether we should go home. By the time we got back to the apartment my mother was not there. I was shocked and confused, and started to cry. There was a note on the table addressed to my father, which stated that my aunt had taken my mother to the hospital.

My father turned on the TV and told me that my mother was going to be alright. I don't know if he believed it, or just told me that to calm me down. We sat there and watched TV for what seemed like hours, but I have no idea how long it was. After that, my father took me outside and we hailed a cab to go to the hospital. Upon entering the hospital, we found my aunt and walked over to her. At this point my father handed me off to my aunt and proceeded to walk away and leave the hospital. I later found out my mother had two cracked vertebrate, and although it was still pretty serious, she would be ok, if ok means having to wear a brace for several months and having several follow up surgeries to correct the injury.

My father had moved out by the time my mother was released from the hospital. Out of fear, or exhaustion, I think he knew the relationship was over. My mother started her recovery, but we were left with virtually nothing. My father was not giving us any money and my mother couldn't go back to work because of her injury. Nursing had always been a career she could fall back on because it was in such high demand at the time, but her body wouldn't allow it for several months. My aunts came to stay and help out during this time, and sometimes I stayed at their houses.

"Wow, in my short time as a counselor I have heard some sad stories, but I have to admit that your story is deeply disturbing and I am sorry you had to witness that, especially being so young. Do you need a hug, Hope?"

"No, but thanks for asking, Mr. Morris. *I could tell he wasn't used to hugging, but probably just wanted to be as supportive as he could be.* Actually, telling that story wasn't as hard as I thought it was going to be. I have cried so many times as I replayed it in my mind over the last 6 years. Maybe now I have just grown numb to the details. Maybe I have reflected on it so much that it became a part of me, of my suffering, almost entering Han territory."

"What is Han? Is that a person or a thing?" *he asked.*

Narrator chimed in. "If I may be so bold to interject. Han is a Korean word and concept which is supposed to be the embodiment of suffering. It is unique to the Korean culture, which has deep roots in the concept of injustice and helplessness. Because Korea was invaded by so many foreign neighbors, the word Han developed as a way to describe this helplessness regarding the people who came under foreign rule and had to endure relentless atrocities. In addition, the word has developed over time to include injustices which occur within the Korean society because of its class system and the hardships which exist within that system. Today, many Koreans use the word to describe sorrow, despair, and pain when confronting life's many problems. It is a word most Koreans today know and understand."

"Thank you, Narrator, *I said*. That was maybe more of a history lesson than I would have given, but it does cover the concept of the word. I have always understood the word to mean a deep suffering. Many in my parents' generation have used it to describe any pain and suffering which occurred in their lives, and the almost built-in expectation of suffering at some point. I am sure some of that idea rubbed off on me, especially as tragic events have unfolded in my life. I wish the suffering didn't come from my family and instead from the world-at-large, but I guess Han has no boundaries," *I said with a half-smile.*

Mr. Morris looked at me with an empathetic smile. "Although I can't completely understand the cultural implications of how you view suffering in general and your own suffering, I feel confident stating that you should never have had to witness the abuse you did and it should never be excused."

"I agree, *I said*. Someday I would like to forgive my father for the way he hurt my mother, but I will never forget. And the concept of Han does not excuse his behavior in my mind. I understand the emotional element behind the word because I feel as if my life has been filled with suffering at times. And I do make light of the concept as I did just a moment ago, but it does feel better sometimes to know that other people have experienced pain and suffering as well. If I think about the word more deeply, though, it angers me, because it originated from suffering which was outside of the control of the people affected. It came from foreign invasions and occupations, civil war, poverty, political unrest, and unfair classism. My father was raised in a privileged environment and a decent family, easily escaping any suffering. He was the one who brought suffering on my mother and our family, instead of any outside force. Joy or pain was within his control."

"Forgive me, *he said,* because I don't want to analyze this one day too much, but it must have had such an enormous impact on your life. How you view your family, yourself, other men, almost everything, must have been affected by what unfolded."

"I know it has, *I said*. I have thought about it so many times. But the weird thing is I wonder what would have happened had it not come to that harsh conclusion. Would my mother have stayed with my father and continued to endure abuse? Would I be ruled by my father and have to show him respect and honor his decisions, even if I had little respect for him? Would I see the world through dark colored lenses and repeat his behavior? All I ever wanted was to be part of a family that loved me. I know I have lost at least half of that love because I am not sure if my father is ever coming back into my life. I know my mother has her problems and makes a ton of mistakes, but I still have some hope for the future. If my parents had stayed together I don't know if I would be hopeful in any way."

"So what was it like after your parents separated and eventually divorced?" *he asked*.

It was ok for a while I guess. My mother slowly recovered physically and was able to start working as a nurse again. Her roles were restricted, though, based on the fact that her injury prevented her from really lifting a whole lot, especially patients. I lived with my mother and my aunts came by from time to time to help out. I saw my father every once in a while on the weekends. He was renting some small, dingy apartment in the city. He barely had any furniture, with only an old couch, chair, and a mattress on the ground. His kitchen was small and it looked as if my father didn't have much food or cooked anything himself. When I came to visit we mostly just hung out in his apartment. I am not sure if he knew what to do with me, or whether he even wanted me there. Sometimes we would just sit on the couch and watch TV, often a symphony, play, or opera he had recorded from PBS. I guess he wanted me to watch those programs to further my high-culture education, or maybe he just really enjoyed them. Other times we would just sit there and watch football. I never really understood why my father would think an 8 or 9 year old girl would want to sit there watching football all day.

And it surprised me that my father was even watching it himself, as it didn't really fit with his interests or personality. Maybe it was a way for my father to try to fit into this American experience. I could see how football was becoming as American as apple pie. Maybe he wanted to go into the office and shoot the breeze with his co-workers regarding the latest football games. Maybe my father had this fantasy that his co-workers would ask him about the games, he would respond with some kind of acknowledgement, maybe they would high five him, slap each other's butts, and then invite my father out for some drinks and pick up some "chicks." I really don't know. I do know he struggled with trying to fit into the American world. The world at home was the Korean world, where we spoke the language, ate the food, my parents would talk about the same things they may have talked about if they were still in their home country. All of their friends and relatives were Korean and they didn't have to bend over backwards to either fit in or figure other people out. But now that world was mostly lost for my father. He and my mother barely spoke. He didn't have many friends, if any, and he really wasn't tied to any Korean community through church or other organizations. So maybe he was making more of an attempt at one world because the other world had faded away.

Even though my father didn't really treat me well, I think I understood him more than I understood my mother. We both tend to think about things very deeply and can both live in our own heads quite a bit of the time. I could see there was a well of information in his head and he was very contemplative and maybe even retrospective. I guess, though, where he fell short was that no amount of contemplation can make up for his lack of action. Maybe my father wanted to apologize to me and my mother. Maybe he wanted to have one of those sit down, cry-it-out kind of conversations where he admitted his flaws and just wanted to be with me and my mother. But either because of his upbringing or personality he was just never able to bring himself to get over those barriers in his mind and heart. Or maybe it was because his heart was not soft enough. I prayed for him and hoped someday his heart would be softened and he would return to my life in some meaningful way, or at least show he cared about me and loved me even if he wasn't around very much.

At that time, though, I wasn't sure if either of my parents really cared about me. It hurt me to wonder whether either of my parents even wanted to spend time with me, and it became more of a question after the divorce. I think I lived with my mother just because it was the norm in America. My mother would often tell me that she was going to send me to live with my father if I didn't listen to her. My father would have been at such a loss about how to raise me, though. He probably thought I needed a higher class education in school and in life in order for me to attain my goal *(really his goal)* of becoming a doctor, but he didn't contribute to my education or direction after the divorce. I lived with my mother, but I was home alone most nights, and would go to camps away from home during the summers. I guess it was rare when my mother and I were actually at home together for any meaningful amount of time. Our relationship was like passing ships in the night, slowly glancing over to recognize the other person without getting close enough to converse.

Many days I would just pray over and over again for a family. When I hung out with my friends and sometimes ate dinner with their families, I would always get so excited. Even if we were eating sloppy joes and the family had weird quirks, it was still the family I never had. I can't remember how many nights I would sit there by myself, alone in our place. Whether I was eating, reading, or doing my homework, I would always have the TV on in the background so it felt like I had a friend with me. I really wanted something different than what I had, even if it was some jumbled and ridiculous family, because at that time my family was really just me and the TV.

Fall

Chapter 5.5: Stuff

The last couple of weeks have been going a little bit better. I felt good about telling Mr. Morris my story. I don't know if I have ever told my story from start to finish to anyone. It was kinda a relief to not have that bottled up inside of me. I know my mother or father would probably kill me if they knew I told anyone, especially someone they thought of as a stranger. Oh well.

I have come to realize that Mr. Lee is a really nice guy. He has been helping me with my golf game, and likes hanging out with me if my mother is busy with her business transition. Sometimes he takes me different places on the weekends when I am not hanging with friends. I haven't told him the history of my family, but I feel as if he understands how much my life has been in upheaval and so he seems to really pay attention to me when we have conversations. Every once in a while he even tries to give me advice about life. It's a nice change to be listened to and talked to instead of talked at. I am kinda curious about his old family and why he decided to leave, but I don't want to ask. Maybe his wife was hard to get along with. I understand that. But I do feel bad for his kids. I wonder if they know where he is and what he is doing. My guess is that his wife made up a story and told them he is away on business, or fighting in a war. How could he possibly be in a war since he is so old, though? Which, speaking of war, because of his name, I have started calling him General Lee, in my head of course. It just makes it more fun to think of him that way.

We moved out of the motel and into an apartment too, which was such a relief. The motel looked like one of those out of a horror movie so I was always afraid to open my eyes at night. The apartment is two bedrooms, so at least I have my own room. So far everyone is getting along. My mother is in the process of moving her businesses to Michigan so she has been pretty busy. But she is home a lot more now, so it is actually nice to see her again. She has been obsessive about running her businesses and making money in the past, so I hope being at home a little bit has reminded her that I should be more important than money. I think she feels embarrassed about the whole running off situation, which is understandable because she acted crazy, but I am at least trying to treat her normally.

I have been trying to convince my mother to take me to a large Korean church in the area. I don't know what it is, but I am craving being around other Koreans, as well as getting in touch with God. Not that I have to go to church to do that, but I would feel so much better being around other people who believe. I know General Lee is trying his hardest right now, but he is not my father. And my real father is who knows where doing who knows what, so I don't feel like I have a father. I guess in these times I have turned to the Lord to be my father. It says in the Bible that He is our father. I don't always feel like He is, but I do try to seek Him out when I think He could be my father and help me get through all this craziness.

My mother doesn't want to go to a Korean church right now, though, because she is afraid someone will find out about her situation and she would feel shame. I know she isn't too far off. All it takes is one person from the church in Michigan to know one person from our former church in Chicago and for them to talk about our situation. Word may spread through our new church pretty fast since Koreans tend to be pretty gossipy. So I do understand her dilemma, but I really need to go. Maybe she will let me go on my own. If only I were old enough to drive myself.

Stacy, Kelly, and I have been hanging out a lot lately, which is really cool. We call ourselves the 3 amigos. It's always a good time with them. We all like to play music and dance. We may even go to a concert in Detroit if one of our parents chaperones. I doubt my mother would do that, and it would probably be pretty uncomfortable for General Lee to hang out with 3 girls. Maybe Stacy or Kelly's moms could take us. There are a few malls in the area so we have been hanging out there on the weekends a lot. We saw some boys we recognized from school and Stacy just yelled at them as we were walking by. They came over to talk to us, which was pretty cool. One of the boys was so cute and I immediately developed a crush on him. His name is Jimmy Knox and he is so cool. He is tall, with thick brown hair, really nice eyes, and dimples when he smiles. He seems pretty confident too, but not conceited or anything. We all walked around the mall for most of that afternoon, just talking and eating junk food. Jimmy was so funny and had a sarcastic sense of humor. I tried to say some sarcastic jokes and do a few goofy things too. I don't know what came over me because I am usually pretty shy. Even Stacy noticed and gave me the thumbs up when Jimmy wasn't looking.

We have seen those boys in school since that Saturday and it has been really cool. I try to think of interesting things to say to Jimmy when I am at home or daydreaming in class. The other day I said, "Hey Knox, does your family own Fort Knox? Can you give me some gold?" He responded, "I don't have any gold, but maybe I can Knox your socks off," and smiled. He laughed as he was saying it and I thought it was funny too. He uses the name Hope a lot when he is goofing around, like "I hope you think I am cool," while emphasizing the word hope. Sometimes he calls me by my last name. He yells out "Hey, Kim, what's up?" in the hall. I know it is more a guy thing to call other people by their last names, but I think it is kinda cool. It is as if we have something special between us, I dunno. I think he is flirting, but I am not always sure. I wonder if he thinks about me when he is alone. Wow, I hope so. I have never really known how to act around guys, but it feels so natural to be around Jimmy. Maybe it is Romeo and Juliet. We have been reading it in English class. I always wondered what it would be like to meet someone and have a connection right away. Maybe Jimmy is my Romeo. I know it sounds silly, but it could happen, right?

Fall

Chapter 6: Romeo and Juliet, Anyone?

"Hope, thank you for opening up and being vulnerable when you described such a painful part of your life during last session. I know it was hard on you and I appreciate the trust. How do you feel after thinking about it?"

I could see that Mr. Morris genuinely cared. "I feel better. I hadn't openly addressed those incidents in my life before so it felt good to finally let it out. I haven't dwelled on it too much. The last few weeks have been really good, so I haven't been thinking about my family craziness as much."

"That's good. What has been going well for you?"

"We moved into a new apartment, a two bedroom. General Lee, as I am calling him now, is turning out to be a really nice guy. Stacy, Kelly, and I have been hanging out a lot. And I met such a cool guy. He is so tall, cute, dreamy, smart, funny. I have been thinking about him since I met him. I feel nervous around him, but for whatever reason my shyness kinda went out the window. I have never really experienced that with anyone."

"That's great. First crushes are always fun, and usually fond memories," *he said*.

"First crush? That is all he will be…to produce fond memories? How do you know it won't be love? I know we are young, and in school, blah blah blah, but Romeo and Juliet were young, right? And they were from two different cultures, just like Jimmy and me."

"I hope you are not Romeo and Juliet, because I hate to burst your bubble if you haven't read the whole story yet, but they both die at the end."

"What about you Mr. Morris, are you and your wife Romeo and Juliet, except for the dying part of course? Was it love at first sight? Is it Romeo and Juliet forever?"

"Uh, I think we should focus more on you. I don't think that is something we should talk about."

"Why not? We are just having a conversation right?"

"Well, there are certain boundaries we should keep during our sessions and for our relationship. You know, from a professional standpoint. Limits among counselor and subject."

"Subject? So I am like a science experiment, like a monkey in a cage?" *I blurted out.*

"Sorry, I misspoke. You are not a subject. But we have a professional relationship. I am not sure I have a suitable word to define you."

"I get it. But are we friends?"

"I guess. We can be professional friends," *he stated very professionally.*

"I am pretty sure if we saw each other on the street we would talk to each other, right?"

"Right."

"So we are friends," *I said with a smile.*

"I suppose," *he said with a guarded smile.*

"Wow, how hard is that? It's not like we are going to start making out just because we are friends." *I could see him blushing and he noticed he was blushing and tried to stop it by adjusting himself in his chair and taking a sip of water. Zip it creeps. It's not like that. It is just cool to see Mr. Morris blush.*

"Hope, you there?"

"Sorry, I must've been deep in thought."

"Even though it is my duty to explore your thoughts, this is one time where I will not ask. What were we talking about again?" *he asked.*

"Your life, your wife, Romeo and Juliet."

"Oh, a subject we should not talk about."

"Come on. You know this will help me. I have horrible role models when it comes to relationships and any insight into healthy ones would definitely help me....you know from a psychological perspective," *I said with a smile. I was hoping I could appeal to his counseling mind.*

"Ok. I will talk about this a little bit. But I want you to know this is a special circumstance and you can't discuss this outside this room."

"No problem," *I said with a giddy anticipation.*

So I met my wife in college. I transferred into my second college as a junior, and met her literally the first day on campus because I attended an orientation for all transfer students. She was a former transfer student herself and in charge of helping us adjust as well as plan a few social activities. Since it was a small school there weren't too many transfers. I attended a few of the social outings like bowling or movie night. I remember her beauty from the moment I met her. She had long flowing red hair, bright green eyes, and a big smile. She laughed a lot and made the world seem enjoyable, which was something I was not used to, being from such a stoic family. On a couple of those social outings I remember standing there with what she later said were blank stares on my face. She also says she has never met anyone who can go such long periods of time without making an expression. I think that is my normal face, but she thought it was odd. So when she saw me standing there, expressionless, during these outings she used to smile at me, or jump up near me, or even do a little dance. I asked her what she was doing and she told me with a big smile that it was her responsibility, as transfer coordinator, to make SURE I was having a good time. I told her I was confused by her behavior and wondered whether she had some kind of condition. She giggled at my absurd thought and wondered why I couldn't just let loose and have a good time. On one outing, we were trading glances throughout the night, and I was working up the nerve to ask her out when one of the other students came up to me and said, "Isn't Katie great. Her boyfriend Josh is a lucky man."

"Josh, hmm" I said.

"Yeah, Josh Goodwin, you know the son of Adam Goodwin, the famous TV preacher and author."

I looked at him with a bit of a blank face. I was a Christian, and grew up in the church, but I guess I was not aware of some of these Christian authors and preachers.

"Adam Goodwin wrote those books on Christian persecution and how to defend your faith in the everyday world," he stated.

It turns out Adam Goodwin was not exactly Billy Graham in his preaching and fame, but wasn't Jimmy Swaggart either.

Swaggart is the popular preacher from the 70s and 80s who was caught with a prostitute, cried for forgiveness, left his ministry, came back to his ministry, then was pulled over driving the wrong way down a street, drunk, with a prostitute in his car, left the ministry…I think you get the gist.

Adam seemed like a genuine guy and someone who only achieved fame based on talent, rather than the empty ambitions of some of the televangelists of the 1980s.

If only Josh was humble and decent like his father. Josh must've thought he was a televangelist as well, always carrying himself with an attitude. He was popular around school because of his name or this confidence he appeared to have, because I don't remember anyone saying how funny, or cool, or nice he was. He seemed to have a blank personality, but tried really hard to be something. It's funny, because the 80s had so many different styles, between the preps, the jocks, the big hair and glam outfits, or the rocker almost-grunge look. I remember Josh not being able to pick and looked as if he tried to be all things at all times, as if he were a caricature, but one which changed from day to day. He was destined to be a televangelist himself, except for his lack of skill, personality, and everything needed to achieve that goal. The school required that we attend a chapel service a few times a week, and they almost never allowed a student to give the sermon. However, with Josh, it was different. He led the service a few times, always looking like someone who had just gotten out of bed, like a homeless person almost, portraying a too-cool-for-school attitude. His speech pattern was bland and he stumbled over his words. But to my amazement, so many students appeared to eat it up. I guess the idea of him and his c-list celebrity was overpowering. He ate it up too, thinking he was something special.

All of that really didn't matter though. The one thing that did matter is that he wasn't a nice guy, and definitely wasn't nice to Katie. They were in their senior year of college and were talking about getting married. He never really looked that into her, though, since he had no room for anyone else after worshipping himself. Josh loved the attention which came from his minor celebrity and definitely loved the attention from other women. In their final semester, Josh went on a mission trip to the South to help build a school for at-risk youth. While he was there he cheated on Katie with another girl from the mission trip. Nothing like cheating on your girlfriend while doing God's work. When he got back to school he didn't admit to the cheating until word got back to Katie. The funny, or tragic thing was that he tried to weave God into his speech about how the cheating happened. Something about how he was praying and God was telling him that maybe his relationship with Katie wasn't right and how he needed to trust what God was telling him. Katie couldn't believe what he was saying to her, but it didn't surprise me that much. I had heard almost the same ridiculousness from a few of the other youth pastor majors, which Josh was. It was always comical to hear some dude try to talk about how through prayer he had come to a decision, or that God was pulling him in another direction, even though he had already cheated on his girlfriend or had lined up another girl to date. And it was just about the best excuse for these guys at a Christian college. Their girlfriends were trying so hard to be mature about it, or forgiving, or respect the fact that maybe these guys were really in touch with the Lord and their enormous faith was causing them to see greater revelations. I couldn't believe anyone would buy into their crazy explanations. Forgive my language, but for all intents and purposes, a few of these guys were about the biggest douchebags you will ever meet, especially when they used God's name to get away with something like that. Hopefully they have matured over the last few years.

Narrator chimed in, "Excuse me, not to make a big issue of this, but I do not believe douchebag is an early 90s word, and as such would not be appropriate to use in this setting."

"How can it not be the right word and I am using it?" *Mr. Morris asked.*

"It is a word which did not become really popular until the year 2000 at least and so I do not believe it would be appropriate in this circumstance."

"Well, how do you know I didn't make the word popular and that I am the first one to use it? Maybe it took a few years to really reach its popularity."

"I am looking at the research and I don't see any reference to David Morris being the inventor of the word douchebag."

"I am. I am inventing it now. Just like in *Back to the Future* you should see the future rewritten."

"That is not how the future works. *Back to the Future* is inaccurate."

"Geez, Narrator, *I yelled*. I wanted to hear the rest of Mr. Morris' story. What are you doing? Can you just let me listen until his story is done? YOU are being a douchebag now."

"What? That is inappropriate language, especially for you Hope," *Narrator stated.*

"He is right, Hope. I am sorry for being a bad influence. Please don't use that language."

"I am sorry, *I said*. Ok, can we all agree to go back to the story?"

"Ok, I am not sure where I left off."

"Josh was cheating on Katie."

"Oh yeah, *Mr. Morris continued*, so they broke up and then got back together and then broke up again right around graduation. I had only spoken to Katie in passing over that year and never told her I was into her because of her relationship being in limbo, or maybe because I lacked the guts. By the time they broke up for good she was already moving on to the next phase of her life and I still had a year left until graduation. I guess I just wimped out on asking her out or expressing my feelings."

"So how did you finally get together?" *I asked*.

I graduated from school and started a trading job at a financial firm in Chicago. I was living downtown and one of my buddies invited me to a party he was throwing because he had just graduated from business school. A couple of our friends happened to be mutual, so I ran into Katie there. Neither of us was in a relationship, and it seemed like old times. Katie started dancing with a few friends (she is a really good dancer by the way), and kept looking at me. I just stood there of course, but glanced back at her. The stares continued until she finally looked right at me and smiled. We spent most of the night talking and I gave her a ride home. I didn't ask her out because I didn't know about her situation, but both of us actually called our mutual friends to ask about each other. Katie got my number from our friend and called me. I finally asked her out over the phone and the rest is history I guess.

"The rest is history? *I asked*. What about dating and marriage? Do you still like being married to her?"

"Yes, I still like being married to her, and I believe she thinks the same way. I know you talked about Romeo and Juliet, but the romantics have to realize that they had a short love before death."

"Yeah, as I read it I wondered what life would be like for them if they continued their romance and had a sorta-normal life. Would it become less cool? Would Juliet become fat and lose her looks and Romeo takes a crappy job and just likes to watch TV? Is that what happened to you?" *I asked with a beaming smile.*

He smiled. "Nope. My wife is very beautiful and hopefully I do more than watch TV. But marriage is hard work and love isn't just a feeling. It is a feeling and a thought, a feeling and an action, a feeling and a knowing. And marriage isn't about just love, as there is a lot that goes into the relationship. We have definitely had our ups and downs, but so far it has been pretty good."

"What caused the ups and downs?" *I asked.*

"Once again, it may be getting a little deep and personal for our purposes."

"What, you are going to stop now? This is supposed to be the part I listen to. It is easy to describe a whirlwind romance, but the ups and downs are the most important, right? I mean, the difference between my parents and a good relationship might have just been their inability to handle the ups and downs, right?"

Ok, I guess I will give you a few examples of the ups and downs without getting into too much detail. When you first get married, it is hard to know what to expect. Most people probably just expect what they are used to, which often involves what they observed from their own upbringing and family. I came from a pretty stoic family where there was not a ton of outward emotion. Her family was pretty expressive and generally told each other on a daily basis what they were feeling about a situation. So when we had any sort of disagreement or difficulty, I tended to just keep my feelings to myself and she would blurt out whatever she was thinking. This led to tension at times because she wanted me to be more proactive with my feelings and thoughts. Outward vulnerability meant love in her family because it showed a level of trust. I often wanted us to discuss things in a very non-emotional way since that was what I was used to. I took a step back when she was pouring out her emotions and often didn't know how to deal with it. Looking back at myself, I was probably not used to having someone cry around me or really show a sense of sorrow outwardly. So it took a lot of communication for us to recognize that our upbringings really affected how we communicated with each other. Most of the time, when two people argue, each person thinks inevitably that the way he conducts himself is the best way, the "right" way, and that the other person is just wrong for even thinking differently. Most couples, I suppose, have to get past the idea of "rightness" when thinking about communication styles, and instead look at it as just a difference. For us, it took a long time to separate issues into two categories, one in which there is an actual right and wrong, and one where we have to find the right style of communication to solve the problem.

"Cool. See…I am learning. Was that too hard? Any other times you had to work through something?" *I asked.*

"Well, in marriage and any two person relationship, you are always working through something. We definitely had different views of marriage going into ours."

"How so?" *I asked.*

Well, I guess I would say, for lack of better words, I tended to be stoic and independent, and she tended to be emotional and needy. Which even now, thinking about the word needy, I know my wife would be rolling her eyes as we speak. I grew up in a house with all brothers where we were taught to be stoic and unemotional. When I came into our marriage, I thought that somehow we would have a similar relationship, where we didn't have to talk about emotional issues if we didn't want to. Marriage, though, is truly a journey, and a challenge-you-to-the-core kind of journey where the end result is two becoming one. It is a process like no other and one that will tear you up if you are unprepared. I had to learn really fast that my wife is an emotional being and I needed to be there for her in the serious times as well as with the day-to-day little things. I had to become in-tune with her in a way that I never was with my brothers, or family, or friends. I had to respond to her in a different way, and at times it was tough. It challenged me to be more thoughtful about her feelings, to be proactive with my love, and to not hide my feelings from her. I can say I am a better man because of it, but it took a while and continues to this day.

"What about her? She can't be perfect, right?"

No, absolutely not, and neither am I. As I stated before, we came from two different upbringings. She was definitely more emotional and expressive when it came to her relationships. And it was an adjustment for her as well. She was used to having people in her family express exactly what they were feeling, and she found it difficult to read me or even trust me if I did not tell her exactly what I was thinking or feeling. She had to come to understand that I was not always going to proactively tell her what I was thinking or feeling about a situation, and she had to be patient with me or at least ask me to express myself. And when I was silent, she had to learn that silence and the unknowing are not always negative. In the past, she perceived that when someone was being silent about an issue, it must be negative. But it is just as equally possible that a person is thinking something positive amongst the silence. She eventually had to trust that in times of silence I still love her as much, am still thinking positive thoughts about her or the situation, and am not running away from her emotionally.

I also believe she thought marriage would be different than what it is. Her parents married when they were young and I think Katie always believed she would be like her parents. She had a perception, at times, that she would not be a complete person until she got married. Yes, a strong marriage will complete each person as they journey through life, but it puts a lot of stress on the relationship to accomplish that right away. The other person is never going to be exactly what you want, never going to make up for all of your weaknesses, never going to rescue you from all of your own angst or fears, and never going to fill in all of the holes in your heart. I think some people believe their life is like a slice of Swiss cheese, and a spouse is somehow going to fill in all of those holes with the greatest of ease. Yes, don't get me wrong, a marriage can be something where two people can be symbiotic, strong where the other is weak, and stronger together than apart. However, those goals usually take years to achieve, a lot of hard work, as well as a lot of challenging and sharpening of each other. I think for my wife, she had a naïve belief that I would be her knight in shining armor, be everything she wanted, and that would never change.

The good, or bad part, depending on how you look at it, is that the first year of marriage is usually like a slap in the face and it will wake you up to your naiveté pretty quickly. If I could come up with a synopsis of our two schools of thought regarding our expectations for the other person, I had to learn and trust that she could help me with my weaknesses and holes which I had in my life and it was ok to be open about what those holes were, and she had to learn and trust that holes take time to fill and it was not going to be an easy process. When the holes are filled, though, with God's help of course, I do believe that two become one. It is a mystery and a spiritual journey, but when things are going well between Katie and I, I really do feel a oneness with her.

I also tend to think of the verse Proverbs 27:17, "As iron sharpens iron, so one person sharpens another." It is based on the fact that if you have two pieces of iron for purpose of farming (like sheers for sheering sheep), or for battle (swords), those pieces will be much sharper as they are rubbed and scraped against each other. They will also be sharpened even better if heat is applied to the process. So, although theory is always easier than reality, a marriage should be like iron sharpening iron. Two people, living independent lives, come together as one, challenging each other, scraping against each other, colliding, and even providing the heat. However, I know sharpening iron is a hard and tedious process. It is not easy, and it is definitely not Romeo and Juliet. Sorry to burst your bubble if that is what you hoped for.

"Trust me, *I stated,* coming from my background I don't think I expect Romeo and Juliet. It's just nice to think of the possibilities though. As far as iron sharpening iron, I think my family sharpened their iron so it would be easier to stab the other person with it."

"Right. I know you were joking a little bit just now, *he added,* but it is true that anytime two competing objects collide, there is always the possibility of an explosion or tragedy."

Fall

Chapter 7: Korean Hillbilly Genius

"Hope, I know it has been a couple of weeks since we discussed serious issues from your past, but do you feel comfortable sharing a little bit more?"

"Oh, I am always ready for sharing, Mr. Morris. Are you ready to be all psychobabbly? Oops, did I say that out loud. That is my word for all of this serious stuff."

"So I sound psychobabbly? I thought I was just a wise friend and adviser. I haven't even measured your head circumference or asked you about your dreams, have I?" *he asked jokingly.*

"Measuring head circumference. I definitely wouldn't do that to me, or other Koreans. *Seriously, don't measure my head.* It takes us a while to grow into our heads sometimes. I used to have the biggest cheeks and head for my body I think. I am so happy I have grown a lot over the last couple of years."

"Your head looks proportional to me, if that is a compliment. *He smiled.* And your cheeks are who you are. You are unique, at least to us white folks. Embrace it."

"Thanks for saying so." *Unique actually sounded positive when he said it. I hope people think I am unique looking and not weird. I hope all of my friends and Jimmy think I am unique too.*

"I know you told me a little bit about your relationship with your parents and life after their divorce. What happened between when your parents divorced and you came here?"

After my parents' divorce my mother tried as hard as she could to support me and herself. She had various nursing jobs and her hours were pretty all-over-the-place, so it left me to fend for myself many nights. I went to school and would take the bus home, which meant I was home alone around 4 pm. If my mother had to work the night shift, I might have to do everything myself, which usually involved making mac and cheese, or Spaghettios for myself, doing my homework, and then watching TV or reading a book. We had one old TV with the bunny ears which only got 3 channels clearly and about 4 others you could barely see. I guess the bunny ears didn't have the power to break through dingy apartment bricks. I always had the TV on just so it felt like I wasn't home alone, but I could only watch so much TV. So I took up reading, lots of reading. My mother would take me to the library on the weekends and I would check out as many books as I could hold in my arms to take home. I loved mystery and fantasy, classics, and the usual pre-teen selection like *Sweet Valley High*. Books became my window to the world. I was confined to a 20-by-20 dingy cell of a place for 6 hours a day, often alone. But with books I could be on an island with unique people, could travel to distant lands, or even lands to be discovered. I could experience what it was like to have a lot of friends and how Americans talked. The history of the world was displayed right in front of me and I couldn't get enough of it. No matter how harsh the real world was, I could read every day and escape my own reality. And the books didn't care who I was. I didn't have to look a certain way, or have the right words to say, or be "cool." They were right there to be read and someone wanted me to read them. As long as I knew English, I was part of the world of books. And my English skills grew and grew as well. My parents spoke to me almost exclusively in Korean, with a few English words thrown in there from time to time. Most of my English skills were learned through *Sesame Street*, other American TV programs, school, but mostly through books. The weird part about gaining language skills through books is that my word choice was very divergent based on the genres I was reading. At the time I didn't realize some characters in books, and the language they used, were more of a caricature than a character. Sometimes I would read the pre-teen and teen books and believed everyone talked like the girls from *Sweet Valley High*. Or I thought all educated adults talked like the Dickens or Jane Austen novels, not realizing the language used was from a different time, continent, and even class. So some of my English vocabulary was stuck between the mundane, almost-silly American style, and the old-timey aristocratic British English.

Even in school I would try to sneak in some reading of my favorite books. For elementary school I attended some pretty crappy Chicago public schools as we seemed to move from one crappy area to another. I was surprised to see so many of these kids in my classes, raised from birth with English-speaking parents, have virtually no grasp of the English language. Sometimes I felt bad for them, but it was hard to endure how slow the day would often seem to me. I remember thinking how it was torturous to sit through class reading time, when every kid read a small section from the book as we went around the room. It took some kids forever, so most of the time I just spent time reading my own books from home. Certain teachers had problems with my outside reading, but most just accepted the fact that I was bored and I needed some kind of mental stimulation.

Starting school in general was such a confusing time for me. I went to some low-rated city schools at the time and really excelled. My teachers all thought I was smart and they were so proud of the kind of effort and results I would achieve. I believe they especially thought it was great that, here I was, an immigrant kid who just learned to speak English from TV and books, and was excelling next to kids who had an extra head start. They would give me cool stickers on my papers and tests, circle my grades, use exclamation points, tell me how much I knew, compliment me on a daily basis, and even hug me when I left for the day. But then I would go home and my father would ask me what I learned in school that day. If I didn't have a great answer or forgot what I learned at that very moment because I was intimidated by him, I would get a scolding. My teacher would circle a 93 grade at the top of my test, with an exclamation point and a smiley-faced sticker next to it. My father would look at the paper and ask me why I didn't get a 100. He would point out the wrong answers and would ask the questions I missed over and over again until I got the right answers. If I didn't get the right answers quickly enough I would get a scolding or maybe even a spanking. He would often justify his stern behavior with a serious question, "How are you going to be a doctor someday with this type of performance?"

I later realized it was the Korean way, or maybe even the Asian way. Talking with other kids with Asian parents helped me realize that. Except for the fact that I was the only Asian kid in most of my classes growing up, so I initially didn't get a chance to talk with kids who had a similar experience.

Education, education, education. Most Asian parents think education is the only way to achieve a better life for their kids. My parents were no different, except for the fact that they were highly educated, and look at them. What were they doing with their vast educations? Why was I living in slum apartments, watching TV which barely came in, and going to terrible city schools? I even gave my parents credit for the idea that education from foreign countries might not translate here in America. Our cab driver could have been a former doctor in Kazakhstan, maybe the grocery clerk had a literary degree in Zimbabwe, maybe the fish monger at the local market was the former UN Ambassador from France. Ok, that's a stretch, but you get my point. So immigrants often shed their past, started from square one, and worked their way up. But my parents seemed to be working their way down, as if there was a basement of life which they hadn't seen yet. As if they were talking to a real-estate-agent-for-life, "Yes, Mam, we would actually like to see the basement of life if you are able to show us. Hmm, I wonder how long we could live in this basement?" So I was caught between two strange worlds. My teachers praised me, my parents scolded me. My parents didn't seem to be working toward a better life, so all the pressure was on me to provide one. I knew English, and even surpassed all of the American kids in my classes, but it just wasn't good enough for them.

Moving to Northwest Indiana with my mother, several years after their divorce, was even stranger. We moved to a place which was only about 45 minutes outside of Chicago, but it was as if it was a foreign land. Most of the people were white, seemed really nice (which was a little weird coming from the harsher city environment), and had some kind of accent. It wasn't really a Southern accent, but it definitely didn't sound like the city. It was sort of a country accent where different words were used with a different speaking style, a different cadence. People didn't appear to be in a rush to go anywhere. No one was running, pushing to get to the right place on the train or bus, or brushing past us on the sidewalk because they "had to be somewhere." People seemed happier and content. They would talk to us at the grocery store or say hi to us if we passed them on the sidewalk. The kids in school were really nice to me, even if they thought I was different. Who knows what they were really thinking in their heads, but somehow they were taught to be nice to others. We were once again living in a dingy apartment, although this time it was more like the middle-of-nowhere instead of jammed in between other dingy apartments, the way it was in the city. And our neighbors were really nice. Because my mother took a job working at a local hospital with, once again, an unpredictable schedule, I was forced to fend for myself. But this time some of the neighbors found out about my mother's schedule and offered to babysit me or allow me to come over to their apartments and hang out. I didn't really dread going home from school anymore because I realized there were people around me who cared about me, or were at least polite enough to feign caring. Either way it didn't matter, because I had somewhere I could go, instead of sitting alone in our apartment. And I discovered tater tots. I don't know what it was about tater tots, but in my mind it was the best American invention I have ever encountered. One of my neighbors used to invite me over after school. She was a single mom with a couple of kids around my age. I would often eat dinner at their place and it seemed as if no matter what meal was prepared, tater tots would be a side dish. I couldn't get enough tater tots.

My father would have been so mad, knowing that we were living in an area he would have thought of as economically depressed, eating tater tots, and hanging out with people he considered lower class. But the people were really nice and maybe they didn't care what class they were in. Maybe they knew they were lower class and were comfortable with it, or even liked it. Maybe they had a chip on their shoulder and had disdain for anyone who thought they were better than them. Whatever it was, these people treated me better than any group had treated me before. And I was really grateful to be there. If only I could have stayed there longer.

There was a pattern in my family where my parents just made major decisions and then told me after the fact. It wasn't that odd coming from a Korean family, but it was a little odd based on the decisions they were making. Most Korean parents of their generation felt it unnecessary to explain to their kids why they did the things they did. Parents told their children how it was going to be and children listened and respected that. There were no long, drawn out conversations the way I observed with my American friends and their parents. But many Korean kids probably didn't find too many things to question when their parents provided them a house, toys, cars, stability. My parents were making crazy decisions with no explanation. "We are moving here, we are moving there, we are divorced, I invite you over for the weekend, I move away without telling you, we are moving to another city, we are moving to yet another city, I am married to another person....what??!!"

Yep, it was sorta like that. I went away to a summer camp for a month and a half and when I came back my mother had married another man, and she was already living with him in another apartment, back in Chicago. No explanation necessary I guess. I was so confused because I don't think I had even met the guy. Maybe I had and totally forgot. Maybe my mother had introduced him as a friend and I saw him in passing. I don't remember though. The only thing I knew was that I was back, they were married, and my life of living in our nice lower-class Indiana environment was gone. The only good thing at the time was that we moved into a two bedroom apartment. Can you believe it?! Two bedrooms. We were really moving up in the world. No more tiny studio apartments filled with rugs where the dirt wasn't so tiny. I even had a bed with a wooden frame and a desk for reading and writing. No more mattresses on the floor, wondering whether mice would eat humans if they were really hungry. The bed in my room was actually a bunkbed because my mother's new husband had a son from a previous marriage. There was a time when I thought we would be a real family. The son didn't visit much, though, since his mother lived far away and it didn't seem as if he had a good relationship with his father. Join the party.

We were still living in a part of town which wasn't the greatest, but it was definitely a step up from any place I had lived before. My mother's new husband was nice at first, so I tried to adjust to this new reality.

My stepfather, which I am reluctant to call him even to this day…actually, I take that back. I am not going to call him stepfather. The crazy thing is that he wanted me to call him father almost from day one of meeting him. So he and my mother date and get married in secret, I barely know anything about him, yet I am expected to call him father? They explained that I should use that language out of respect for him. Yes, Korean male respect must trump logic. I would have loved to respect my real father, and even this person, but I found it hard to respect either of them. At least my father garnered some official title because I am a product of him and he is on my birth certificate. I guess I am more American than I thought because I am questioning my parents and making them "earn" my respect. Totally an American concept. I doubt many Koreans, or Asians for that matter, believe that their parents need to earn their respect. Oh well. So out of disrespect for him I will refer to him as

Korean Dude Number 2. That has a nice ring to it anyway, doesn't it?

So Korean Dude Number 2 was pretty nice to me at the start. I started going to a private junior high. No more crummy city schools for me. Korean Dude Number 2 was a businessman who was growing his retail business when he met my mother. I don't know if it was his plan from the start, or he just fell into it, but his sense of retail seemed genius. He started with a store which sold shoes, athletic gear, and clothes in a rougher neighborhood. Once that store became profitable, he would put another store in another rough neighborhood. Once that store became profitable he would repeat the pattern. It turned out that his method really worked. He paid less rent, was the only store of that type around, and surprisingly some of the rougher neighborhoods had residents who spent substantially more on clothes and shoes, even if they had much lower incomes. It made sense if you were to tour some of these neighborhoods. Everyone was wearing the latest Air Jordans, the newest Starter jackets, the coolest new NBA hats, the latest jerseys from some of the star athletes. And all this money was going into Korean Dude Number 2's pockets.

My mother seemed pretty happy too. Korean Dude Number 2 bought her clothes, jewelry, and even a Mercedes Benz. My mother even took me shopping for all new clothes before I started back to school. And she wanted to make sure I had all the best labeled clothes at the time. I was really happy at that moment. I figured I would be wearing the coolest clothes even if my face didn't fit in.

My mother and Korean Dude Number 2's whirlwind romance seemed to go pretty well for about a year. He provided for her and me, continued to expand his business, and even helped my mother open a jewelry store of her own. My mother paid for my tennis lessons, golf lessons, and even horseback riding. Yes, horseback riding. I don't know if they expected me to enter the Olympics in the equestrian events, or just thought it looked classy, but I took riding lessons. Even my father would have been proud of the class of lessons I was taking. I never understood how riding around on an animal, wearing a silly hat and outfit, makes a person classy, though.

I was really getting into my schoolwork and starting to enjoy it. Kids at school had a lot of ignorant and racist things to say to me, but I tried my hardest to fit in. My mother and Korean Dude Number 2 were really busy with their businesses and were never around. At first, I went back to the kid home alone, eating Spaghettios while watching TV, and reading a lot. But then more opportunities came my way to break out of that mold. I joined the cheerleading, basketball, and volleyball teams during the year. I realized I was pretty good at these sports and it gave me confidence. I actually met some friends, too, and they started to treat me like one of them despite the fact I was the only Korean around. My mother and Korean Dude Number 2 never went to any of my games or events, so I was pretty hurt and bummed at first. But then I realized they were never going to come and at least I had a chance to do all of these cool activities. I found out several years later that most of my Korean and Asian friends weren't allowed to join as many activities as I was. Because so many Korean parents are obsessed with education and schoolwork, they often didn't want their children to join many extracurricular activities because it took away from their studies.

My mother and Korean Dude Number 2 were so focused on themselves that they really didn't even ask me much about school. I got good grades so they never cared what else I was doing. That was strange to me because my father's expectations regarding my education were at odds with what I was doing. But by this point he was almost completely out of my life. I barely heard from him and didn't even know where he was living.

Year two was when Korean Dude Number 2 and my mother really started down a bad path. I began to hear a lot of arguments between them. My mother was growing her businesses and was not around very much. Neither was Korean Dude Number 2, so you would think they would enjoy spending time with each other when they were together, but it wasn't the case. My mother and Korean Dude Number 2 came from different backgrounds in Korea and definitely different classes. Korean Dude Number 2 lacked the formal education my mother had and moved to America because he didn't have much of a future in Korea. He would have been someone who was working in the fields with a dirty neck and dark tan. It is crazy to think about, because so many people in America spend all summer trying to get tans, but having darker skin in Korea sometimes indicated that a person was in the lower class because he labored outside all day. So Korean Dude Number 2 appeared to fit into this category in my mother's eyes. Even though their English skills were about the same, his Korean was not as well-spoken and his accent didn't sound as proper. When my mother and Korean Dude Number 2 went to social outings with other Koreans, my mother would often appear embarrassed by him. Sometimes she would tell me that he was, in the closest English translation, a hillbilly. I wasn't really sure what to think of her opinion at the time. I felt bad for Korean Dude Number 2. He helped me and my mother out of poverty, provided us with nice things and I was going to a decent school. My mother started her businesses with his financial help and knowhow and they were now starting to do well. But somehow now he isn't good enough because he is a hillbilly?

It all seemed pretty silly to me. It was as if my father had been turned on his head and placed inside this guy. My father was well educated, well-spoken, came from stature and money, knew the correct manners and words to impress other Koreans at a dinner party if necessary, but had us living in filth, on food stamps and free food, raged against my mother, and didn't provide me with any help for my future. Korean Dude Number 2 was poorly educated, poor-spoken, from nothing in Korea, supposedly couldn't impress other Koreans in certain social settings, but was providing lessons, cars, clothes, schooling, and a genuine future for my mother and me. But he was a Korean hillbilly. It was as if my mother and her supposed Korean friends were trampling on the American dream. The American dream was here to provide anyone in the world a chance to achieve something that they couldn't in their own country. And hard work and ingenuity allowed a person to pass whoever was above him on the class scale in as little as a generation, or even a few years. Korean Dude Number 2 had done that. I think most Americans would really respect a guy like that. But these other Koreans weren't letting him outrun his past and his class, and neither was my mother.

Their arguments started to get worse over the next year. I tried to stay as busy as I could with school and other activities, but even the small amount of time I spent at home became excruciating. Maybe my mother didn't need Korean Dude Number 2 anymore now that her businesses were doing well. Maybe she was grateful for his help in lifting us up, but never really liked or loved him. Maybe he had a sense of that. The arguments became more personal in nature where my mother really did go after his past and did accuse him of acting lower class. He thought she was ungrateful and a snob, and really wanted her to see how great his achievements were. He wanted respect, and she wasn't going to give him the respect he was looking for. My mother really knew how to twist the knife in these arguments, and taking away a Korean man's pride and respect is generally considered a low blow.

And so Korean Dude Number 2 started treating me worse as well. My father had taken it out on my mother when he felt he couldn't stand up to the world. I think Korean Dude Number 2 took it out on me when he felt he couldn't stand up to my mother. All of a sudden he started to question my behavior, yell at me for little things I did around the apartment, and wanted to stop paying for all of my lessons and extracurricular activities. Maybe it was his way of getting attention from my mother because it did appear as if she was starting to ignore him. The arguments started to diminish somewhat, and my mother barely spoke to Korean Dude Number 2 anymore, and almost avoided him at all costs. Of course she couldn't avoid him at night, so I always wore earplugs to bed just in case they decided to start an argument.

The final blow was near the end of that second year. I came home from volleyball practice, grabbed a snack from the fridge, and plopped down on the couch to veg out in front of the TV. I noticed that my mother's bedroom door was shut so I yelled out to see if she was home. I heard no answer so I assumed she was still at work. About 20 minutes later my mother came out of her bedroom and walked over to the front door to make sure the deadbolt was locked in addition to the lock on the door handle. It seemed odd to me based on the fact that we only used the deadbolt lock at night. I later found out that Korean Dude Number 2 had called my mother from his car phone and was a couple of minutes away. Maybe he wanted to see if there was any dinner prepared or whether we should go out for dinner. Whatever was said, my guess was that Korean Dude Number 2 could sense there was something off, based on my mother's words or her demeanor.

A few minutes passed and I heard a banging at our door and Korean Dude Number 2 was asking if someone could let him in. After a few seconds he started taking out his key and turning the door handle lock. He was still banging at the door and by this time was yelling for someone to let him in. My mother burst out of her bedroom and told me to put the chain lock on the door. I asked her why and she just yelled at me to do it. I started to have flashbacks of my father and I thought maybe Korean Dude Number 2 was going to hurt my mother, so I went over to the door and put the chain lock on just as he was unlocking the deadbolt. Korean Dude Number 2 pushed the door until it caught on the chain. There was enough space between the door and the frame and I was able to see a portion of his face. He was peering into the apartment and saw me standing there. He yelled at me to open the door. I froze, but then glanced over at my mother. She was standing a few feet outside of her bedroom door, but was looking into the bedroom. A few seconds went by and I just yelled out "Mother!" Without looking at me she just told me to wait there. I looked over at the door and could see Korean Dude Number 2 looking right at me and yelling at me to open the door. He told me he was going to kick in the door if I didn't open it right away. A couple more seconds passed and I looked over towards my mother's bedroom, when I saw a man hurriedly walking by my mother with no socks on, a shirt on, boxers and pants which were half pulled up. He was trying to hold his shoes and socks in one hand while trying to pull up his boxers and pants up with the other hand. My mother pushed him over towards the window near the fire escape. She opened the window as wide as she could and he took one step half way out and then tumbled onto the fire escape. Within a few seconds he was running down the steps, his boxers and pants starting to slip down as he descended.

Then came a pop sound as Korean Dude Number 2 was able to use his shoulder or leg to bust the door in and break the chain lock. He ran over to my mother and started screaming at her and telling her that he knew what was going on. She was standing right by the window and attempting to block his view. He pushed her out of the way and stuck his head out of the window as far as he could and looked down. It appeared as if he was unable to see anyone because he froze there for a few seconds and turned his head left and right. I thought maybe it was over and he was going to calm down, especially if he didn't see anything. But hillbilly or not, he was not that stupid. He pulled his head back in and turned to my mother and started yelling at her. She attempted to stand her ground and act as if he was being crazy and making things up. He pointed at me and asked my mother why I wouldn't open the door for him when he was asking and then yelling at me to do so. My mother didn't answer. So Korean Dude Number 2 almost ran over to where I was standing and screamed at me that I had better tell him the truth. I didn't know what to do and was looking at my mother for help. She didn't provide me with an answer and it looked as if she wasn't going to take responsibility. He screamed at me again. So I just lunged forward and started running for the nearest room, which was the bathroom. I tried to shut the door behind me as I ran in there, but Korean Dude Number 2 was right behind me and pushed the door open. I ran and jumped into the shower and attempted to close the curtains. He slapped the curtains out of the way with one hand and started to raise his other hand. I crouched down a little bit and put my hands over my ears and attempted to shield my upper body with my elbows. He started slapping me in my back and legs and anywhere he was able to get a clean shot. He was yelling, but I was concentrating so much on trying to deflect his hands that I didn't even know what he was saying. My mother ran into the bathroom and started yelling at him to stop. After a few more seconds she grabbed his arm and managed to make his hand miss my body. He stopped and looked right at her as if he was going to hit her, but surprisingly just yelled, "I should be hitting you." She just yelled back, "You are crazy, what is wrong with you?" He stared at her for a few more seconds, red in the face and his eyes as wide as can be. Then he turned and walked out of the bathroom and then headed right out of the apartment.

My mother tried to console me by grabbing me for a hug, but I just pushed her away and yelled, "What have you done, what is your problem!" I rushed into my bedroom, slammed the door, and buried myself on my bed. I started to cry like never before. My mother came into the room, but I just turned to her and yelled, "Get out!" She put her head down a little bit, turned toward the door, and walked out. I kept crying until I almost couldn't cry anymore, and then I whimpered for a bit while I stared off at the walls. I was in shock and couldn't digest what had just happened. Korean Dude Number 2 was argumentative with my mother, but he never seemed to have that kind of temper. And I couldn't understand why he was hitting me. I would never want him to hit my mother, but he had to have known I was just following her orders. I went to sleep that night hoping this was just a blip, a fluke, a mistake, but I knew yet another major change was coming my way.

My mother tried to apologize to me for days and weeks. I didn't even want to listen to what she was telling me. Sometimes she would try to say that Korean Dude Number 2 was a bad guy and someday I would understand. Or that grown up matters are too complicated for me to understand. Oh, I understood. I had sex ed by that point in my schooling, and I knew Korean Dude Number 2 hit me instead of hitting my mother. He probably felt he was punishing her more by hitting me. I was the sacrificial lamb and my mother never really acknowledged the pain I endured for her. I knew it wasn't fair at all. And I must've known in the back of my mind any hope of a real family and some stability was gone.

That day wasn't the official end of the relationship, but it was the end. Korean Dude Number 2 and my mother tried to reconcile over the next couple of months. Neither person really apologized for anything, but it appeared as if they made an attempt to make something work. They went out alone at night on a few occasions and were at least polite with each other in the apartment. I didn't really hear any arguments so I thought maybe they had patched things up.

After school was out for the summer, my mother sent me to summer camp. I was able to escape all of the weirdness between Korean Dude Number 2 and my mother for a while. I was hoping that by the time I got back their relationship would be better. When my mom picked me up from camp I asked her if things were good between her and Korean Dude Number 2. She responded with a kind of non-answer, "Sure, things were going ok." When I saw them together for the first time, they were pretty cordial to each other, so I was hopeful they were back on track. A few days later, though, is where the craziness ensued. Upon getting home from hanging out with a friend, I went to my room and saw that it was almost empty. All of my posters were gone from the walls and all of my trinkets were gone from my desk. I looked in my closet and nothing was there. I looked through my drawers and they were empty. I went out into the living room and yelled for my mother. She told me to come with her. I asked her what was going on and she told me she would explain later. We went out to the parking lot and I could see our car was packed to the brim with stuff. I saw a man standing there as if he were waiting for us. He introduced himself as Mr. Lee and told me that he was going to travel with my mother and me. I was surprised, confused, but maybe not stunned. I was pretty sure Mr. Lee was the one I saw jumping out of our apartment a few months ago, so things started to make more sense as I stared. I couldn't even think of anything to say so I just stood there. My mother told me to get in the car and I did. I was becoming an expert mover and so this incident didn't seem unusual to me, as if I expected it. I took one long glance back at the apartment building knowing it would probably be the last time I see it, as well as Korean Dude Number 2.

"Hope, I know I keep saying I feel incredibly sorry for everything that has happened to you, but

I am. It must have been so painful to move around all of those times and then to have your mother put you in a position where you were hit by a man. I tried not to interrupt because I wasn't sure what to say and wanted to let you tell your story."

"Thanks, Mr. Morris. Usually I can come up with something funny or amusing to say which will help break the tension when I recount certain parts of my life, but I am at a loss. For me, this hurt even more than the fights with my father and mother. It wasn't because I was the one getting hit this time, either. I think it is because I at least understand my parents' fighting and my father's rage more so than this incident. My mother and father had a very complex relationship involving their upbringings, their immigration to America, careers, visions, supporting a child and how to raise me, and ultimately how they treated each other. The tension was building over years and their behavior was changing with the tension. Here, my mother and Korean Dude Number 2 seemed to fight over class status, and ultimately cheating. It came quick and powerfully. I did not have enough time to process it. I thought it was more simplistic than what I saw with my parents, which made it more hurtful I guess. I can understand that complex problems need complex solutions, so maybe my parents didn't have a complex solution and it ultimately led to the end of their relationship. But this situation involved what I thought was a simple solution to a simple problem. And my mother couldn't deal with the simple solution before it blew up."

"Do you not blame the man you call Korean Dude Number 2 for hitting you?"

"No, I blame him. I no longer make excuses or try to justify the abuse from the father figures in my life, but I do try to understand where the rage is coming from. Maybe it was just a matter of time before Korean Dude Number 2 was going to explode. Which is why my mother never should have been with him in the first place. But it felt different this time. My father would strike my mother for less serious, almost trivial reasons by the end of their relationship. Korean Dude Number 2's rage was definitely provoked by a serious incident. So I will never forgive, or at least not forget, Korean Dude Number 2's actions, but I am still mad at my mother for provoking him."

"I understand what you are saying. Do you think your mother's actions represented some sort of regression?"

"Yeah, I think that is pretty accurate. Before then, I knew we had hit bottom after my father left. The relationship with Korean Dude Number 2 seemed to provide a lot of positives, and many aspects of our life felt like they were going in the right direction. I am afraid my mother will sabotage things if they start to go well again, even if no abuse is involved."

"I get that. It comes down to trust, and especially trust for the future," *he said*.

"Totally. I want to be able to trust and hope for the future."

Winter

Chapter 8: Duality of Man

"Hope, So how are things going since we last talked?" *Mr. Morris asked.*

"Really good actually." *I had a smile on my face.*

"What has changed?"

"Well, remember how I was telling you that my mother was afraid to go to the Korean churches in the area because she was concerned someone there would know about her past and that she would feel shame. I had been trying to convince her to go for the last few months for her sake as well as mine. No matter what I said, though, it looked as if she wasn't going to listen to me. But the other night I finally blew up at her and got really mad. I told her I needed to go to church, and I needed to be part of a Korean community. I explained to her that even though I have made a few friends in school, it just doesn't feel the same unless I am around other Koreans every once in a while. She saw how upset I was and finally relented. We went to church last Sunday at a large Korean church and then I even went to the high school youth group meeting last Tuesday night."

"That sounds great. How do you feel?" *he asked.*

I feel great. I met some new people right away. It felt like a familiar face, literally and figuratively, like a warm blanket. During most weeks there is a pot luck meal before the meeting and so I chowed down on some really good Korean food. Maybe it is a Korean thing, or cultural thing, or immigrant thing, but food is sometimes the antidote to hardship, the commonality between friends and family. Food is such a big part of our lives and eating it provided me such a comfortable feeling. Other parents brought bulgogi, kalbi, spicy soups, banchan, and always kimchi. No one thought the food was weird or the smell was too strong. It was home to us and it felt like home to me. Even though I am so Americanized now, Korean food always brings me back to my roots. It was especially exciting for me because my mother rarely cooks anymore, and when she does, it isn't even Korean food.

Since I was the new kid, I actually got a little bit more attention than I was expecting, but it was good. And of course no one looked at me because they thought I was so different looking. My eyes looked just as they are supposed to look, my nose wasn't too flat, my cheeks weren't too big, and I wasn't too short. In fact, I am tall for a Korean girl. I even thought a few of the boys were checking me out during the meeting. There were even a few girls who gave me their numbers at the end of the meeting and told me that they usually hang out after church on Sundays. Hopefully they weren't just being nice and we could actually hang out some time.

I left the meeting feeling pretty good. It is always nice to feel like you belong without actually trying too hard. I have learned the American way, I think, and have started to do better in school settings and being in the ultra-minority, but it is nice to know I didn't have to figure out anything for this meeting. I knew how to act, what food we were eating, and I understood how others interacted. My mother isn't exactly the typical Korean parent anymore, but my father was more traditional, as was Korean Dude Number 2 and some of my other family members. So it was not a stretch to be around others who were raised in a similar way with similar attitudes.

"Cool. I am happy for you. Do you think you are going to continue to go to church and youth group?" *he asked.*

"I hope so. I think I will spazz out at my mother if she tries to prevent me from going. If she doesn't want to show her face in church because of her fear, then I will at least beg her to let me go alone.

I know I am going to sound as psychobabbly as I make fun of you for sounding, but I think I need that second world to fall back on. No matter what happens in school with my other white, American friends, I will feel more comfortable knowing there are Koreans my age who will accept me for who I am and will understand where I am coming from. And the flipside may be true as well. I know some of my cousins, and Korean friends from the past, who are so secluded within the Korean community that they have not branched out for fear of being around different people and cultures. I know I am different from the traditional Korean teen because I have always been immersed in American culture. So if there is ever a time where the traditional Korean environment becomes too stale or comfortable to me, then I always have the more challenging, but possibly illuminating American culture which I have a love/hate relationship with."

"I think the points you made are very mature and you have a deep understanding of the two worlds you are struggling between, *he added*. Have you ever heard of the concept of dualism?"

"No, I don't think so."

"I won't go into all of the details, *he continued*, but since you were talking about two worlds, I thought it might have some bearing on our conversation. The concept of dualism has been studied by philosophers and psychologists for hundreds of years, and although it mostly has to do with the mind/body distinction instead of dual cultures, it may help you when thinking about how to approach your life and how you are sometimes caught between two worlds.

The basic premise is that mind and body are separate, and therefore divided into two categories, mind and matter. I am sure you have heard the phrase 'mind over matter'? Well, in a very simple way, that phrase is showing the interconnection between this duality. There are many theories as to how the mind and body interact, as well as the spirit. So there is a duality between the mind and spirit as well. There is also the objective and subjective nature of ourselves, with objective being tied to physicality and subjective tied to the mind or spirit. If I continued to delve into the reasoning I am sure it would be boring or confusing, but I can say that as we mature, especially as teenagers, dualism is ever present. How we feel relates to how we act. Do our minds and spirits control our actions, or do actions control our minds and spirits?

As a mental exercise, I would like you to come up with examples of distinct differences or even opposites which exist in your life. You were talking about the two worlds, relating to the

Korean and American culture. What are some attributes which make them different?"

"Korean culture, *I stated*, is so much about family, where parents are to be respected and children are to learn and follow rules. American families seem to have some rules, but the ones I have been around really value their kids' independence and like the fact that the kids even voice their own opinions. Korean culture is very homogenous and community focused, where American culture seems to reward individualism and eccentricity. I think a pattern I have seen amongst Korean families is where the parents sacrifice everything for their children, or at least tell them that over and over again, and what the children do for their parents never seems to be good enough. It is a tough concept to understand for many Americans I know. For me, I understand the concept even though my parents haven't always fit that mold. The parents may have come from humble beginnings, or at least some generation in their family did, and they always want their children to succeed, so they can have a better life than their parents. So they push their kids in school, in music, in just about everything they do. They can be so hard on their kids. In return, the kids are supposed to understand the type of sacrifice their parents are making, respect that sacrifice, and therefore dutifully carry out their parents' requests, commands, goals, and ultimate visions. I have seen this work for many families, but I also know it causes a lot of stress and pain at times. I have witnessed cousins who were more independent minded, and therefore disrespectful in their parents eyes, and paid the price through extreme punishments. But I have also seen relatives who were really successful in life, and probably would not have been without their parents' pressure. On the opposite end, I have seen American parents who are really strict with their kids, and some who are really laid back. I am not sure if there is a better method. I have seen kids thrive in either environment, or head down the loser path in both. It is all very confusing for me to try to generalize American culture, because I don't think there is one. And moving around so much in the past 6 years has convinced me that American culture can change dramatically if you travel just a few miles."

"Those are good examples of different views as you see them in your life. What about how you think and act? How about when there are hard events in your life, as there have been many so far. Are there opposing ways you think about when handling certain circumstances?" *he asked.*

"I dunno, exactly. I know it pains my heart to think of so many of the things which have happened to me already. Sometimes I sit and cry because I believe it will be better if I get it all out and really feel what I am supposed to feel. Other times I try to think of something joyful or funny. Often, I have tried to train myself not to care because I know I will get hurt if I care too much about my life, or my family, or new surroundings. Sometimes I wonder how much of my mother and father are within me, which is kinda scary. My parents are definitely distinctly different in many ways."

"What scares you about your mother and father? What differences do you think about as it pertains to them?" *he asked.*

Sometimes when I lie in bed at night I think about what I might become in life. I ponder whether I will be able to take all that life has to offer. I wish I were in a place where I could just run free mentally and not have to worry so much about whether my life will continue to be in upheaval. Although on some days I feel as if my mother has the right answer, and running away to somewhere and something new seems exhilarating. Maybe she has been running away from boredom and monotony since my father left. She played the role of Korean mother and housewife perfectly for so many years and it resulted in failure and disappointment. She always wants to be good at something, to feel important, to feel as if she matters to those around her and her surroundings. When she was a mother and housewife, she did a good job, but did not receive any praise from my father or others because she did what was expected of her. After my father left, there was no expected path, so she was free to run where her mind and ambition took her. Maybe now her retail business, or making money, or being desired by other men is some kind of accomplishment. It is definitely not the Korean way, and I don't even think it is the American way. Maybe my mother is her own person, and the shackles have been removed. I guess the only problem is that she is running wild with what seems like no guidance or training. Even wild horses usually run in herds. My mother has no herd, whether it be from the Koreans or Americans, and so she is left with no boundaries.

My father, on the other hand, never broke out and allowed himself to run. He purposely stood in place with no realistic goal in sight. Being able to see a goal, but never having the introspection or fortitude to accomplish it left him bruised and angry. His rage grew as he could not break out of his self-imposed cage. I wonder if I will have the courage to really pursue my goals in a realistic fashion, and be ok with failing. I know I will fail, but I hope I continue to get better in whatever I do. I know I have anger inside me, just like my father, but I don't think it has ever grown into rage. I am angry at my parents, but also get angry at my classmates and others who treat me so differently because they can't understand me more deeply, choosing only to look at me with a focus on the surface. What if I feel trapped by my own inadequacies and feel rage growing inside me? I guess I could feel the rage coming on like my father, and then run like my mother.

Maybe that is the answer. Except for the fact that I can't physically pack up my stuff and go, so I can't run like my mother. I guess those are the opposing forces which go on in my head when I think way too much.

"Hope, I am actually blown away by your thinking on this subject. I can't imagine anyone having such profound thoughts about her circumstances as you have just stated to me, especially at such a young age. I actually worry you might think too much, but working through whatever affects us is the only way we grow. I know it comes from deep hurt, but I am really proud of the way you approach what has been forced upon you."

"Really? I mean, there are definite moments when I know I think way too much and I should just be some silly teen, having dance parties with friends. How do people my age generally deal with situations such as mine?"

"There is no particular way young people deal with it, but it can often involve destructive tendencies, *he stated*. There is a great likelihood that teens coming from overly stressful and dysfunctional environments lash out as a way of dealing with their pent up frustration and aggression. Instead of contemplating the impact of their situation, as they may not even be in touch with their emotions or thoughts, they act first to soothe their minds or spirits. Which brings me back to my original point regarding dualism, and mind over matter.

The biggest issue I see with teenagers is the inability to cope, to train the mind and spirit during really tough times. As incomplete beings with brains which aren't fully formed, teenagers desire quick resolutions to their angst and anxiety, or pain and sorrow. But the mind is tested beyond its limits because if it can't control the spirit. And I would argue that teenagers' spirits are more hyperbolic, with higher highs and lower lows, within a short period of time. Which is hard on the mind, because more tests and referendums on the mind can cause fatigue and eventually lead to mental breaks or inconsistent actions. So every day cannot be a test of the mind, nor can it be a challenge to the spirit, as it can be too fragile. This life is long, and the mind and spirit need constant breaks from the daily grind, and from each other for that matter. It is precisely why so many studies show how exercise is good for the mind. Love is good for the mind and spirit. How can this be if we are only physical beings? Mind and spirit must work together to fight through the tough times and enjoy the good times."

"Ok, Mr. Freudy McFreuderson, *I joked*, I get that it helps to not put too much pressure on the mind and spirit, and everything needs to work together, but I am not sure if you know how hard all of that is. I find it so hard to control my emotions when something goes really wrong. Also, isn't that reaction authentic? Aren't the people who just sit there and take it the ones who aren't being truthful with themselves? At least I admit it really sucks sometimes and then try to deal with it. How am I supposed to deal with the worst times?"

"I don't have a perfect answer, *he said*, and it sounds silly, but sometimes life is about survival and sometimes it is about surthrival. It is your job to figure out when you need to hunker down and get through it and the times when you can thrive.

It is ok to flee from a situation mentally or spiritually and find refuge, and put our mind, spirit, and actions into compartments. We often have to ignore areas which may be negative and drag our entire self down. When it is safe to allow every part of ourselves to work together, we can see and experience something in all its glory with our entire body, mind, and spirit."

"Heavy stuff, *I stated*. I wish I could figure out how to do the things you are saying. I guess if I think about it hard enough, maybe at times I have done what you are telling me to do. I dunno. So this duality concept, it seems pretty hard to separate my mind, spirit, or body into compartments, and possibly train myself in mind over matter. Am I supposed to become a different person when bad things happen to me?"

"No, not in the way you are thinking about it. The opposites you mentioned regarding Korean and American culture will hopefully serve as a good starting point."

"How so?" *I wondered.*

"Ok. You are one person of course, but do you think and act differently when you are in an all-Korean environment as opposed to an all-white environment?"

"Yes, I would say that I do."

"But you aren't lying or faking it right?"

"No, I am not faking it in either environment."

"See Hope, this just represents how you can be the same person, authentic, but think and act differently in two different situations. Both of them are you, but you have freedom to think and act as the situation allows it. So many psychologists and philosophers struggle with the concept of opposites in the personality, the duality, as it may indicate instability. But it can also be used to compartmentalize a person's life or to truly embrace those vastly different parts of themselves or experiences. In the same way we can train our minds to think differently depending on the situation and especially the stressor. And in separating our mind and spirit for a time, we are able to prevent action until we have contemplated the consequences to our entire self. Even Jesus himself had to separate his mind and spirit during his most trying time on Earth."

"Jesus?" *I asked.*

"Absolutely, *he continued.* When he was set to be crucified he went to pray by himself, kneeled down and cried out to his father to ask whether there was any way to prevent his harsh death. He knew he had to die, which was his mind knowing the outcome, but still had the presence to express his spirit by crying out with profound emotions. He was in deep agony, and had previously told his disciples of his deep sorrow upon knowing his death was imminent. He knew the path he must take, but still anguished about the human pain and suffering he must endure. Even in the last moments of his life, as he calls out 'Father, why have you forsaken me?' it is a moment of pure spirit. His mind and spirit then act as one as the act is done.

Obviously, this example ends in crucifixion and death, but my point is that we are complex creatures who have the ability to separate our minds or spirits, in order to achieve an ultimate goal. We are the only creatures on this earth who know we exist, essentially allowing us to separate our minds from our spirits and engage in self-reflection. It allows us to grow and change as human beings."

Narrator chimed in, "I would just like to add that I believe apes and dolphins, as well as a few other creatures have self-awareness."

"Why would you say that?" *Mr. Morris inquired.*

Narrator explained, "Scientists put a mark on an animal's body and then place that animal in front of a mirror. The fact that they are able to recognize the mark as being on their body and then study the mark more closely or even touch it shows they have self-awareness."

"Ok, that is a pretty low bar for self-awareness, *Mr. Morris said.* I think what we are discussing is much more complex than what you are referring to. Is a dolphin able to contemplate his existence and then decide whether his mind and spirit are acting in unison, or determine that his mind can control his actions?"

Narrator answered, "I am pretty sure. The Navy even uses dolphins to detect bombs underwater, and you have to be pretty smart to detect bombs."

"Ok, Narrator, you are ridiculous, *I said.* Why would dolphins agree to detect bombs underwater, with no protective suits or devices, if they were so smart? Try getting humans to do that without paying them a gazillion dollars. Even then, most humans wouldn't volunteer for that, unless they were crazy. So are dolphins crazy?"

"Maybe dolphins are very sacrificial and want to better humanity, which is why they risk their lives," *Narrator stated.*

"So now you know how dolphins feel? You are crazy, Narrator," *I said.*

"Also, *Mr. Morris added,* mankind was made in God's image, and therefore has all the attributes of God, including a complex structure where our mind and spirit can be separate, or act as one. Are dolphins made in God's image?"

"I do not know. Why not?" *Narrator asked.*

"Because they just aren't," *Mr. Morris answered.*

Narrator questioned, "Well, if God made everything, and at least some in his image, like humans, who is to say that everything is not made in His image, including dolphins. Maybe God looks like a dolphin at least some of the time, or maybe He looks like a dolphin to dolphins only."

"Ok, now you are just hurting my brain. Hope, is there a way to send Narrator to his room or something? How do you deal with him when he starts down these roads?"

"I do not go to my room. I am not a child."

"I usually just tell him to shut it. He understands that. So shut it, Narrator. Why don't you go swim with some dolphins and you all can contemplate your existence together."

"Ok, you are in charge, Hope. I will keep quiet."

"Doesn't seem that way." *I do need a narrator room.*

"Ok, we got a little side tracked there. What did we learn about the mind and body today?" *Mr. Morris asked.*

"That I know I exist and shouldn't disable bombs?" *I said goofily.*

"Nice." *Mr. Morris was laughing.*

"No, seriously, *I said*. I get it. It is a lot to take in, but I believe I can try to think about the mind and spirit and can essentially separate the two out when needed so there will be 'mind over matter.' I guess it will allow me to control my actions, and temper, and at least give me a break until I am ready to act. Can you give my parents some of these lessons while you are at it? Maybe write them a letter when you get a chance?"

"I know you are joking, but I would encourage you to talk with your mother about some of these ideas and maybe it will help your relationship with her and she will possibly pick up some pointers as well."

"Seriously? You know my mother doesn't even know we are having these sessions. And if I come in talking all psychobabbly to her she might just think I am crazy and pull me out of this school."

"You have never told her? I suppose I understand why, but I am still surprised."

"Maybe when I am all 'centered' and 'self-actualized' I will tell her," *I said with a smile.*

"Ha ha, very funny. Ok, I will let you off the hook on this one. A last point I will make about dualism, and mind over matter is that there are ways to put the mind and spirit at ease, or possibly give them strength to deal with the harsh realities of life. Some people take up hobbies, or exercise, or anything else which allows them to take a break from reality. Is there anything you do to exercise your mind in a healthy way, or at least take a break from reality?"

"Well, I do play tennis and golf, and am going to be on both of those teams. I guess I hang out with friends and try to socialize. I still read a lot as well. Sometimes when I am really feeling down I write poetry."

"Those sound like healthy activities, *he said*. In regards to the poetry, would you mind bringing some of it into our sessions and reading it? We could discuss it as well if you are up for it."

"I…mean…ok, maybe. I dunno. I have never really shown anyone my poetry and it is not really good, I think, or meant to sound good. I just kinda do it when I am upset or even when I am just feeling deep about something. I don't know what good it would do us. I think it would embarrass me because I would want it to be good."

"I am sure it is really good. But it doesn't matter anyway. Incomplete thoughts and incomplete works are good for working through something. The act of doing something and expressing yourself is the main key. And maybe then I can know more about your mind and spirit as you read some of your poetry. I am not going to push you if you don't want to, but I think it is a good coping technique which we can explore."

"Ok, I will think about it. Plus, I know Narrator is looking over my shoulder when I write so I get kinda weirded out. Maybe if he didn't act like that my poetry would be better."

"What are these accusations? *Narrator whined.* I can promise you that I will only read the poetry you ask me to."

"Ok, it is agreed then. I think it will be good. Trust me," *Mr. Morris said reassuringly.*

Winter

Chapter 8.5: Other Stuff

The last few weeks have been going pretty well. Stacy, Kelly, and I are still the 3 amigos, I met some new friends at church, Jimmy and I talk whenever I catch him at the mall or during school, and the sessions with Mr. Morris are helping me think about life in a different way. Kelly's parents invite me over for dinner just about every day, and I take them up on their offer a few times a week. I really like hanging out with them because they are such a cool family, and so at least for that small window of time I feel like I am part of a family. And Stacy opens up a lot about her struggles with her parents' divorce and how her relationship with her dad is still pretty non-existent. For me, it is nice to have someone who is going through the same thing there for me. I get a chance to be there for her, too, which I am not used to. So Kelly and her family provide me with some positives, but Stacy helps me limit the negatives. Maybe I am becoming like Mr. Morris and have started having all of these theories, but I think Stacy likes guys so much and the attention from them because they fill in the hole left by her father. I dunno. I just get the feeling that she needs a guy around, instead of wanting to have a guy around. When we are talking with the boys in our little group, Stacy is way more aggressive than usual lately. Sometimes it even seems like she is flirting with Jimmy, which is weird because she knows I like him.

We went to a Depeche Mode concert last Saturday, which was so much fun. They came to Auburn Hills, which is not that far of a drive. My older cousin took me, Stacy, Kelly, Jimmy, and Jimmy's friend Doug. I am really into 80s music even more so than 90s music. It could be that my older cousins like the 80s music, so I gravitated to it because of them. I also like the fact that 80s music feels more upbeat and sillier in nature. I do like the dance music so far in the 90s, but the grunge is a little bit hard to take. I know I am supposed to relate to the angst and anger of the grunge style, and who better than me to understand, but it depresses me too much. Everyone appears to have a good time when they listen to 80s music. The concert was no different. Most of the people were older, but I didn't mind. I love to sing along to all of their songs.

The drive back from the concert was cool too. My cousin was driving their family's minivan so that everyone could fit. Stacy, Jimmy and I were all sitting in the back seat together. Jimmy was sitting between us and had his arm resting on the back of the seat most of the time. Then all of a sudden he shifted in his seat and let his arm fall and his hand landed on mine, as mine was just resting on the seat. It seemed like a mistake or he was unaware that my hand was there in the first place. But then he just left his hand there, on top of mine. I wouldn't technically call it holding hands because the bottom of his hand was resting on the top of mine. I didn't really look at him for the rest of the ride, as everyone at this point was quiet and restful. He didn't move his hand though, and it must've been another 15 minutes before we finally dropped him off. There was never any acknowledgement on his part, but he must've been attempting to hold my hand in some weird way. Maybe he is just as nervous to mention that he likes me as I am for him. Maybe he likes me, but doesn't "like me like me." I dunno. I guess for now I will take a partial hand holding any day.

Speaking of "liking liking," I think one of the guys in my youth group at church really likes me. His name is Joseph. He is always trying to talk to me and one of the other girls told me that he told her that he likes me. He is really funny, smart, and good looking. He is Korean, which is comforting at times. I am not really sure what to do. Maybe I should listen to Mr. Morris, and get into that whole duality stuff. When I am in the white world, I can date Jimmy and enjoy all the cool things about him. When I am in the Korean world, I can date Joseph and enjoy all the cool things about him. The two worlds don't need to collide, especially since we go to different schools. Sounds like a plan. I wonder what Mr. Morris would think?

Narrator interrupted, "Not to speak on behalf of Mr. Morris, but I do not think he would approve of your plan, or the use of the duality concept to carry it out."

"Got it, Narrator. It was more of a joke. You probably need to date two people at once just to increase the odds of one of them liking you."

"Ok, that is not funny. I happen to be very pleasant to hang out with."

"Oh, what was that? Oh, sorry, I was falling asleep already."

"Ha ha."

Oh, yeah, and another positive is that my mother is going to church with me. I guess she is over her fear of public shaming, or hopefully she knows she needs to be with God as well. I feel bad, though, because she doesn't bring General Lee with her. To me, this is a sign of confidence in their relationship and how serious it isn't. Although I guess I can understand where she is coming from. I mean, how would she introduce him, as her boyfriend? She is old and he is way old. Seems kinda silly. Like, "Hey other person, meet my boyfriend, Mr. OldyMcOlderpants." As much as I like General Lee, old people being girlfriend and boyfriend is gross. But I don't know how she can hide him from the entire Korean community. It is not as if they only attend church. What if my mother and General Lee went to the movies? Maybe some other Koreans would catch them making out in the theater. Busted. Although I guess my mother could tell people she was giving him mouth-to-mouth since General Lee is so old.

I know I am young, and I don't understand adult circumstances, blah blah blah, but I never understood how my mother and General Lee were going to work out anyway. Are they just going to agree to get married? What about their divorces? Will they be in front of the pastor and he asks them to repeat their vows after him, "I solemnly swear to divorce my spouse today and take your hand in marriage now." Then everyone eats some cake. I wonder if she had a ceremony with Korean Dude Number 2 and didn't invite me. Probably not.

Anyway, I really do like General Lee, but I know he has another family. I am torn. At least I enjoy being around him and think he is a good guy.

Winter

Chapter 9: God and Anger Shake

"Mr. Morris, so I know in our last session we talked about my poetry. I am still really nervous to share it, but I did come up with a few poems based on how I have been feeling at times."

"Great. Of course, as I stated before, you have to trust me that I will not embarrass you or think any different of you because of your poetry. I am glad you are willing to express yourself in this manner. I take it Narrator didn't get in the way too much?"

"Starting in on me this early? I resent that," *Narrator stated.*

"Yo, chill out Narrator, *I said*. Just a joke. I will actually compliment him and state that he acted like a perfect gentleman."

"Thank you, Hope."

"Ok, here goes…" *I could feel my heart beating in my throat. I have never shown anyone my poetry before. Maybe I am silly or this poetry isn't any good. Maybe I shouldn't have agreed to do this.*

"It is ok, Hope. Trust me." *Mr. Morris encouraged.*

"Ok…"

An Answer

I call unto the sky
I call unto the sea
I call unto all living things
But no one answers me.

I feel so sad and mourn
On top of a lonely hill
I feel so depressed and miserable
These thoughts I cannot kill.

The silence is thick around me
No comfort is at home
And I know what has to be
I must forever roam.

I cry out in despair
"Oh God, why don't you care?
Sorrow won't ever leave me!
My life is so unfair."

God listened to my loud complains
A light came from above
And God asked so tenderly
"How do you not feel my love?"

"If only you'd open your eyes
Then you would clearly see
The one special way to happiness
Is yours and yours is the key."

Slowly I opened my tight-shut eyes
And only then did I see
That all my words were foolish cries
As joy surrounded me!

The bright-eyed birds chirped gaily
As I returned home
And I looked up and saw God
Smiling from his throne!

I learned life isn't dreary
I learned life isn't sad
And if you don't enjoy life
You only wish you had.

"That is a really good poem, Hope, and I am not just saying that to say it. It is really good, very eye-opening and well-written. I mean it," *Mr. Morris said.*

I still felt a little apprehensive, but I am so relieved he feels this way about my poetry.

"It appears based on your poem that you are feeling pretty good and more positive about life. Is this true?" *he asked.*

"Not really, actually. I feel if I don't put anything positive in my poems about God and life, then somehow I don't believe in His power or it will be difficult to have hope for the future. And it sounds silly, but I don't want you to believe I am some sort of sad case and I go home and have all of these dark thoughts."

"I don't think that about you. I want you to be honest with your feelings, though. Even if you are angry at God, or don't know why He doesn't answer your prayers, I want you to express that. You can't hide from God, and hiding from yourself will never work either."

"Have you ever been angry at God?" *I inquired.*

"Yes, of course. Very angry at times."

"What caused that anger?"

"Well, I am not sure we should get into that. I can just say it is very common to get angry, even very angry at God, no matter who you are. It is perfectly reasonable and normal," *he stated.*

"But I really want to know, *I said*. I think it will help me. Sometimes I walk the halls of school, looking at the faces of the other kids, and I wonder whether they have had good lives. Have their parents treated them well? Did they get the bike they wanted for Christmas? Do they have parents who tell them that they love them every day? Maybe they have brothers and sisters who are really cool, or maybe they have a bunch of friends who really care about them. But I know they might be hiding some sadness too. Maybe they have had it hard at times, but I just don't know them well enough. And if they can seem happy, or at least well-adjusted, then maybe it would help to hear how they get over things or deal with their pain. Maybe hearing your story will help me realize that I am not alone."

"Well, I guess if it will help you that much, I will tell you why I have been angry, *he said*. I don't know if I told you before, but I am an identical twin."

"Really, cool. Are you guys close?" *I asked*.

Yes, we are close, well…were close. It is weird when you have an identical twin because it is a mirror image of yourself. And Daniel and I were no different than most twins, being almost inseparable. We did almost everything together as kids. Liked the same toys, riding bikes, skateboarding, and really loved to play sports. We had the same sense of humor, liked really silly, ridiculous jokes, and to play pranks on people. And it was especially easy to play pranks on some people being twins. We even liked the same types of girls in junior high and high school. Sometimes it became weird because obviously one of us had to get the girl unless we dated twins. But even in our competitions we got along. We played basketball and baseball in high school and were offered scholarships in both sports to some small Division I colleges and other smaller schools. It wasn't until college where there was a divergence between the two of us. I really wanted to play sports, get away from home, and was into political science and criminal justice. He became interested in psychology, wanted to stay close to home, and really didn't want to play sports anymore. I ended up going to a smaller college to compete in sports and pursue my polisci and criminal justice degree a few hundred miles away. He went to a small Christian college near home to pursue psychology. We were apart for our first two years of college, and we definitely grew apart during that time. Before we left for school we would hang out every day, talk all the time, and still rely on each other for so many things. It was probably mostly my fault, because I really wanted to gain this "independence" when I went away for school, but we started to talk on the phone less and less. I often said I was too busy to visit him at his school, and sometimes he would come to visit me but I think he could see there was something different than the way it used to be. Maybe I just wanted to see what it would be like to be on my own, and

Daniel was the biggest reminder of what my old life was like. Daniel went home and visited our family a lot, and I tended to stay away. Even during the breaks I would usually stay with friends or go on road trips. By our sophomore year of college, he had found a really cool girlfriend who would later become his wife. He seemed really peaceful and happy with his new girlfriend and his studies. He wanted to become a counselor at a social service organization to help those in need. He really had a passion for it, even by that age. I, on the other hand, started partying a lot, seeing a lot of different girls, and wasn't really into school. Even playing sports didn't seem that interesting to me anymore.

"How come?" *I asked.*

I don't know. I think I wanted to do whatever went against my upbringing, my family's sort of robotic fashion, and really wanted to break out. Even being a twin might have had an effect on me because I saw my brother falling into line and I really wanted to reject that. But as my sophomore year went on, none of these break-out actions really made me happy. None of the girls I was with compared to Daniel's girlfriend. I wasn't really that passionate about school. And sports had been something we loved to do together, and I lost one half of my team. I guess I didn't know how different it would feel until he wasn't with me during that time.

So I ended up transferring to the school Daniel was at, which was actually a weird thing to talk about with him at first. We had done everything together for the first 18 years of our lives, and I guess I took for granted how much I missed him and needed to be by him. But when we talked about it I wouldn't admit how hard it was and I just said I was transferring. By that time maybe I needed him more than he needed me, but I was okay with that.

Because they didn't have the majors I previously studied, I ended up picking psychology because of the psych credits I already had, and I figured Daniel and I could take some of the same courses together. I didn't really have a plan at that point, but it was cool to be back together again. I still played sports, he still didn't, but the fact that he would come and support me made it fun again. We hung out almost every day again, although I did give his girlfriend and him some space. She was really cool with it, though. I think she really got the whole twin thing and was able to understand the bond. And of course I did end up meeting Katie, although she was not in the picture until a few years after that.

We graduated two years later, but he stuck around to get a master's degree in counseling and I decided I would like to do something more exciting and challenging. I took a low level job in a financial services firm in Chicago and he stayed in Michigan. Although it seemed as if I were running away again, this time I had a different view of my separation from him. We talked just about every day and I really tried to maintain the relationship even though I was away from him. Plus, he and Grace were practically engaged by that point, so I knew they were probably going to start a life together.

He finished his degree and took a job as a social worker in Detroit, working in some of the roughest areas of the city. He loved it and it seemed as if he couldn't get enough of helping others. He and his wife even opened up a free counseling clinic at their church, which they both worked at during their spare time. Daniel became the best person I knew. I, on the other hand, fell into the big-city-trader lifestyle for a little while. I really started to do my homework at the firm and could understand trading and all that it involved. For me, it was like another competition and I loved the adrenaline which came from winning. Within a few years I was making a lot of money for my firm and for myself. I went out with my friends, partied a lot, and really wanted to live a work-hard-play-hard lifestyle. Daniel would often counsel me, because he was a counselor of course, that I wouldn't be able to keep that lifestyle going for very long. And he would often talk about the people he would help on a daily basis and how they lost their way. I think he believed I was going to lose my way at some point. But I didn't see it that way, since money and friends seemed to shield me from becoming like the people he was helping.

I would donate some money to his organization from time to time, but I really didn't think that much about the people he was helping. Sometimes when he told me these stories about the people he helped, I would just think they were lost causes. Daniel was so compassionate, though, and didn't seem to get tired of helping even the "lost causes." To me, I felt as though Daniel was wasting his talent and that many of his clients were just taking advantage of his good heart. Sometimes I would tell him as much, but he would say something like, "You can't be taken advantage of if you want to be taken advantage of." For him, this was his ministry in life.

After meeting Katie again, I did settle down in regards to my partying and friendships, but I still loved the competitive world of trading. Sometimes Daniel would encourage me to pursue other interests outside of work, and even said that if I got a counseling degree then I would be able to volunteer with him and Grace. I figured I would just give money to his clinic or organization, but I did take a few night classes in counseling over the next couple of years. Maybe it was a way to be closer to him, and understand what he dealt with at his work, but I never intended to help others. We did start to have more conversations based on my classes and his work, so I did feel we bonded more during that time. But I still did not feel what he felt for others. I just couldn't be him, couldn't get in his shoes, his head, his heart, to understand why he had such a passion for others. In a way, I didn't understand it. We weren't raised that way. Our parents taught us to run from our emotions, or bury them deep down inside. Daniel was actively searching out for other people's emotions on a daily basis, and then storing them up and confronting his own. When he would talk to me about how he felt about others and their situations, it was as if he was me, but a foreign me I couldn't understand. I could almost picture myself in the mirror talking in a foreign language and I had no idea what the words meant. But I admired him so much and felt as if this was the place for him. I was genuinely happy for him in every way.

Katie and I got married a few years later. Daniel and Grace had a baby girl around that time, which the whole family was happy about. They got married pretty young and both really wanted a family. Daniel and Grace were open about the fact that they had been trying for years to conceive, but it just wasn't happening for them. We didn't pry as to the reason, but we knew they felt devastated about not being able to start a family. They had actually started the initial adoption process when Grace found out she was pregnant. They had their baby girl 9 months later, and then almost right after Sarah was born it happened.

Mr. Morris paused for a long time and his eyes started to well up just a bit. "What happened?" *I asked.*

Daniel was diagnosed with advanced colon cancer. He had been losing a little bit of weight before then, had some pains in his gut, changes to his bowel movements, but he just chalked it up to stress and nerves about having his first kid, as well as any stress from work. He just kept the symptoms to himself for a few weeks or months and then finally told Grace about them. She encouraged him to go see a doctor, but he didn't want to take away from any baby planning and getting the house ready for their daughter. He promised Grace that if he was still having issues after Sarah was born he would go to see a doctor. Neither of them thought it was serious, though, since he was still really young. After Sarah was born, Grace and Daniel really focused on their daughter and just getting through the days. It wasn't until a month or so later that Daniel complained about some pain in his gut and Grace insisted he go see a doctor. His doctor ran some initial tests and the results appeared pretty normal.

But the doctor decided to send him for an MRI just to rule out anything more serious. Even at that point no one really believed it was serious. A couple of days later they were referred to a specialist who uttered the word "cancer." It was colon cancer and had already spread to other areas of his body.

The prognosis wasn't good, but to my surprise Daniel and Grace were so resolute that he was going to beat it. They thought it was a message from God, and it would be a blessing when he was healed. Daniel and Grace both did so much research on his cancer, saw the top specialists, and researched every clinical trial under the sun. Daniel was willing to take whatever treatment was available, no matter how hard and aggressive it was. Grace became almost a doctor, knowing everything there was to know about his cancer. And the prayer, wow the prayer. Everyone from their church was praying, family members, people who Daniel worked with, clients he had helped and found out about his condition, complete strangers who were friends of friends. It was as if Daniel was the most popular guy in town. He had a footprint which was so large and everyone was pulling for him. Daniel didn't shy away from his cancer either. He announced it right away to family, friends, co-workers, church members. It was going to be a testament to his and Grace's faith that he would be healed in the end, against all odds. Even I thought it must be part of God's plan, because he wouldn't let the best person I have known die so young. My guess is everyone else felt the same way.

Daniel fought his cancer so aggressively, and early on it appeared as if it was working. He took the most painful and aggressive treatments, but never really got down on himself. He continued to work full-time, volunteer at their clinic, and be a great dad to Sarah. Daniel would even continue to counsel and encourage me about my life, believing I was the one who needed help. When I heard him pray, most of the time he wouldn't even pray for himself. It was as if he were already healed and other people were the ones who needed prayer. He was so sure and faithful that it made me believe everything was going to be alright. There were times where the information they received from the doctors was positive and everyone really believed he was on the path to beating it. I guess it was around a year-and-a-half into his battle when things started to go downhill. The treatments stopped working, Grace found new treatments and clinical trials, but none appeared to be the answer. Everyone kept praying, Daniel kept believing. The telling sign for me was when Daniel took leave from work. It was his passion to help others, and he knew he didn't have the strength to help others anymore.

Even in the midst of his body deteriorating, though, he continued to pray for others, and write encouraging letters to friends and clients in need. I could feel the disappointment and anger building in me, but he had a peace about him and never seemed to get angry. Through the end he just continued to give to others. Even his last act was a sacrifice. He started to get weaker and weaker, and I think he knew his time was short. But he must've had a goal to make it to Sarah's second birthday. Daniel wanted all the relatives and friends visiting to celebrate and focus on Sarah. You could see his joy and excitement that entire day. Even when people tried to turn their attention to him because of how he was feeling, he quickly shifted their focus by talking about Sarah and her special day. I think he felt a true peace on that day and maybe his mind and spirit told his body it was ok to let go, because he passed away the very next day.

Mr. Morris' eyes and cheeks were red, and a few tears were running down his face. He would glance out the window and then to the corner of the ceiling almost as if he didn't want to look at me or just needed a place to rest his focus. I wasn't sure what to do or say. Should I try to hug him or ask him a question? Maybe I should say something. I should say something important, or profound, or whatever. What should I say to him? Maybe something positive about family or church or something… "I can't imagine how hard that would be. I'm guessing your family and church were a help at that time?"

"I guess in their own way they were a help. But I was so angry and distraught that I probably didn't take their help very easily. I know most people meant well, but I was just too angry to deal with anyone."

"What made you angry?" *I inquired.*

It was just so unfair. Here my brother was a believer, the best person you will ever know, spending all of his time helping others, just had a daughter they had desperately wanted, ready to start his life with Grace and Sarah, his whole life ahead of him, and he was taken away. All the prayer, all of his sacrifice, meant nothing. He would have been the best testament to the healing power of the Lord the world had ever seen. He would have shouted it from the rooftops, gone to work and shown people what it was like to overcome insurmountable odds, able to show clients what it is like to live through pain and end up better on the other side. What more could God ask for? He left a wife, and a child who will never really remember him the way he was. Sarah will be filled-in by videos, pictures, and by us, but she will never experience him the way all of us were able to.

I had this pain and anger which couldn't be satisfied. Daniel and Grace belonged to a strong church, and many of those people were around to help out during that time. Believe me, some of these people were the best in the world, but sometimes my anger grew when I was around them. So many of them always seemed to have the "right" words to say, those supposedly comforting words. The words were supposed to explain it all and hand it over to me all wrapped up in a nice box. There were verses thrown out about how life is fleeting, and we are like blades of grass, or lilies in the field and that our time is short, but eternity is forever. So somehow Daniel dying young wasn't so bad when you consider how long eternity is? How Daniel was such a testament in his time of pain, he had never lost faith even when the inevitable was upon him, he had sown the seeds with his courage and he had died with such dignity.

The dying with dignity idea really got to me. Maybe it was because I never truly saw someone die before, but seeing my brother that last day made me wonder how death can ever be truly dignified. Maybe it was easier for me to see because I was his twin, as I could truly see any difference between him and me. Both of us were 6 foot 2 inches and usually around 200 lbs on any given day. Both of us liked to work out and stay active in our free time, and Daniel was in pretty good shape before he was diagnosed. By his last day he weighed about 100 pounds. You could see all of the bones in his face pretty distinctly, his cheeks were sunken in, still bald from the last chemo running through his blood, eyes yellow from jaundice. His ribs were protruding almost through his skin and his back was hunched a little bit as if his shoulders could no longer hold up his upper body. His legs were like toothpicks and his knee bones popped out because they looked twice the size of his lower thigh muscles. He had no butt left and his hip bones jutted out as the skin stretched around them. This once strong man, my twin, my mirror image, needed help getting up from the bed, needed help walking even with a walker, needed help wiping his own butt after going to the bathroom. His daughter by this point was too heavy for him to hold, sometimes even while he was sitting up. She had to be placed right next to him so that he could lean her against his side.

On his last day it seemed as if he felt better. He wasn't eating very much on a daily basis by that time, but asked Grace if she could get him some breakfast and appeared ready to eat just about everything. He didn't end up eating very much, but the fact that he wanted to eat felt like a good sign. He called a few of us into their bedroom to hang out and watch some football. A few hours later he said he wasn't feeling well and started vomiting. But since everyone was used to this level of nausea and vomiting no one really thought this day was any different. He needed to go to the bathroom, but started getting dizzy when others were helping him get up. Everyone instructed him to stay in bed. Daniel was embarrassed because he told everyone he had to poop and he would prefer some privacy. Everyone left the room except for Grace and I. By this point Grace was so used to everything related to his cancer that she didn't even bat an eye. They didn't have a bedpan, but she got some hospital pads and placed them under his butt. She caressed Daniel's head and told him it was ok and not to be embarrassed. Daniel went poo and what came out was a really soft green poo. Grace went under the cover, cleaned him up with some wipes, and placed another pad under him. Then five minutes later another poo, very green in color. Grace went under again, cleaned him up, and another pad. Then a few minutes later another one. This seemed to go on for almost an hour. Sometimes he would vomit at the same time, so I held the vomit pan under his chin as he threw up. Grace gave him something for the nausea, but it didn't seem to help. Daniel said he felt like he needed to get all of this stuff out of him and then would feel better. His breathing started to change, though, and he felt some discomfort in his chest. Grace gave him a morphine pill to relieve any pain and to hopefully slow his breathing down a little. Grace was the resident expert now and I think she had a feeling it might be the end. But Daniel and

Grace had an agreement that she would not signal to him if she sensed it was the end, because Daniel just wanted to live every second without thinking about death. It wasn't as if my brother wasn't aware he was going to die, but he lived every day day-by-day, moment-by-moment, and I think he wanted to continue that philosophy even until his last moment on Earth.

Whether or not it would be a signal, though, Grace briefly stepped out of the room to encourage everyone to come back in. I sat next to Daniel in a chair holding one of his hands and Grace lied down on the bed with him, holding his other hand. Daniel then said with a faint smile, "Once I feel better tomorrow we will have to finish putting Sarah's doll house together." Someone had placed Sarah next to his leg by this point and he looked at her and then Grace. Everyone just nodded and smiled, trying to hold back tears. No one had any profound last words to say and they sensed Daniel wanted to die thinking of tomorrow. His breathing became a little more labored. He sat up and threw up a little. He kept pooping into the pad which was below him. Whenever Grace had a free second she cleaned him up and put another pad down.

He didn't say another word as his breathing became more labored over the next several minutes. Grace asked if he could hear her and to squeeze her hand if he could. He squeezed her hand, but had a guttural sound from his chest and it seemed as if he was struggling to breathe. Grace finally propped herself up a little bit so she could see into his eyes and told him, "It is ok to go, Honey. Sarah will be ok. I will be ok. You have done so much for our family and this world. It is ok to let go. Everyone in this room loves you so much." Daniel gave one last look up at her, shed one tear, and his eyes rolled back into his head. He was comatose, but continued to breathe. Grace whispered loving words into his ear for the next 30 minutes until his body finally took its last breath.

The whole time Grace was whispering to him I sat there, clenching his limp hand asking God why He had to let Daniel die. Why did He let such a wonderful, loving, compassionate, and sacrificial person die? Why didn't I die instead of him? Daniel was the better twin. He was the one who poured his life out for others, the one who had constant faith, the one who never doubted God, the one who prayed consistently for others even in his dying days, the one who sacrificed by reaching out to others as he wasted away. He was my mirror. We have the exact same DNA and he got cancer instead of me. God gave cancer to the wrong person. Daniel was the one to save the world.

Dying with dignity? A man devoted to God, vomiting and pooping every ounce of bile and liquid in his body while he lie dying. How is that dignity? How is that special and spiritual?

Mr. Morris paused, his face still red and his eyes still full of tears. I wasn't sure what to do. With all of my painful moments in life you would think I would know exactly what to say or do, but I was just frozen. I looked at him as he collected his breath and relaxed a little bit. He sat back in his chair. "Mr. Morris, I am so sorry Daniel died. Are you ok? Do you need a hug?" *I said with a half-smile. He smiled at me politely.*

"Thank you, Hope. I think I will be ok. It is always hard to tell that story, and sometimes I leave out certain details because I know it will make some people uncomfortable. However, I thought you could handle hearing some details because of the intense times you have had in your life and how open you have been with me about those instances."

"Thank you for sharing, Mr. Morris. I know this may sound wrong, but I think I may trust what you have to say in these sessions a little bit more since I know you have had tragic circumstances in your life. I respect the fact that you understand pain, and it is not just some theory in your mind. If you don't mind me asking, has the passing of Daniel ever made you question your faith?"

There have been days when I was not sure what I believed anymore, *he said*. How could there be a God and let this suffering take place? How can murderers and rapists live long lives and my better-self die the way he did? It was really hard to work through. I know Daniel would not want me to turn my back on Christ, but I was so angry. Sometimes church members would say something like, "Well, it was good that Jesus suffered because he showed us he was human and suffered in death as well." It is true, Jesus Christ did suffer before he died. Whipped with leather and glass, crown of thorns, had to carry his own cross, nailed to it, stabbed. It certainly is a lot of suffering. After hearing so many people mention Jesus' suffering in death to me, though, I actually said to one of them, "You know, I know Jesus suffered physical pain upon his death, but it is true that some cancer patients probably suffer more physical hardship during their illnesses than Jesus ever did during his death." The look I got was one of bewilderment, mixed with an almost scowl, as if I had said the most blasphemous thing ever mentioned. My point was not to diminish Jesus' sacrifice, but simply to show them that there is suffering in the world just as bad. And what did that person suffer for? He isn't getting credit for saving the souls of humanity. What purpose did his suffering bring? Daniel knew suffering. He listened to his clients' problems on a daily basis...the broken homes, the physical abuse, the gang-infested neighborhoods, the murder of loved ones, the foster kids who no one wanted. He lived with suffering on a daily basis and then still had to suffer in death. He received no reprieve from suffering.

Some days, though, I know my faith is stronger. Not necessarily because I feel any stronger, but because I have made a "choice." The easy answers are gone and I choose to follow God even in the presence of suffering. My head and my spirit are on the same page because I finally made a choice, not from upbringing or ignorance, patterns, or lifestyle, or wanting to believe. It is a choice from the ground, the dirt, the mud, having gone down and experienced and seen human suffering and been forced to choose whether or not to lift my head up.

It is funny, or sad, I guess, but Grace and Daniel were really struggling with whether to continue treatment as Daniel's body started to deteriorate and the cancer got stronger. Grace had lined up clinical trials in the past and had another one almost approved and ready to go a month or so before his death. Daniel wasn't sure if he wanted any more treatment, but he would change his mind from day to day. Grace didn't want to push him too hard, but had been his coach throughout his entire illness. Sometimes they would get upset at each other because they weren't on the same page. So they reached out to the church elders and pastors to see if they could help counsel them on making a decision. Each pastor and elder appeared to have a different answer, but they all sounded pretty confident. God was working this way and that way, healing could come through treatment, or God would heal without treatment, or being at peace and not making any decision was the right way to go. Grace and Daniel both felt an enormous amount of pressure because it was the hardest decision they would ever have to make. Why didn't they agree with each other? Why was no answer clear? Did they not have as much faith as the elders? Why did the elders have such a confidence when Grace and Daniel were so unsure?

Then something changed the nature of this relationship between the elders and Grace and Daniel. A few of the elders and their wives came over to hang out with Grace and Daniel one night. It was a night like any other night in Daniel's cancer battle. Grace made a different dinner meal for Sarah, and Daniel, and herself. Sarah had become a picky eater so she was eating only kid-type foods, and Daniel was only interested in certain foods now because his palette and appetite had changed, and what he wanted changed almost minute by minute. After dinner she had to clean up, do the dishes, change Sarah's diaper, help Daniel to the bathroom, help Daniel to the couch, turn on the TV to a favorite show of his, give Sarah a bath, get her ready for bed, bring Daniel additional food or drinks as he needed, and the list went on. The elders were there to witness this barrage of tasks while they hung out with Daniel. Daniel started getting nauseous and needed something to throw up in. They called for Grace, who ran downstairs while holding Sarah, grabbed a garbage bag and held it under his chin. She placed Sarah down and stroked Daniel's bald head. She could see he was getting sweaty so she grabbed a cloth she had stored in her front pocket and wiped the moisture from his head and face. She nonchalantly talked about the TV show to Daniel and continued to see if Sarah needed anything. Some of the elders by this point were a little uncomfortable and got up from the couches and chairs. A few even wandered into the other room, as if vomiting in front of them was causing them extreme discomfort. Once Daniel was done with this round, Grace tied the garbage bag up and threw it away, then took Sarah upstairs to put her to bed. A few minutes later someone yelled for Grace to come downstairs because Daniel was nauseous again. She was surprised because everyone in the room had just witnessed all of the actions she took. They knew where the garbage bags were, could have gotten a paper towel to wipe Daniel's head and face, and could have talked to him while he threw up. But I guess no one had the comfort level to do those things.

What was interesting is that after that night, none of the elders seemed to have the answers about what to do, or at least were not as confident anymore. I think they recognized the hardship of really being in a battle of life and death and that theories, clichés, and verses don't have all of the answers. And if God really does work in mysterious ways, shouldn't we be humble enough not to presume to know all of God's answers. It is like a history geek who loves to talk about wars and battles, but can't stomach to watch real war footage if it shows death up-close. Reality is usually much harsher than theory, and the reality causes us to question our decisions, or even our deeply held beliefs. So many Civil War buffs seem like nerdy guys, the last people you would want to fight with you if you had to actually go into battle. Would they have been able to help saw their fellow soldier's leg off with a hand saw and no anesthesia because infection was setting in? In life, I have learned, there is always the idea or theory of reality, and then reality itself.

My brother Daniel didn't see war, but he saw human suffering every day and still chose to go back the next day. He didn't shy away from the harsh realities of this world and still chose to worship the Lord and keep a positive attitude. He faced down a dismal prognosis and a harsh cancer without anger or despair. I am stronger when I think of his example and I try to be him. That is the only thing which has gotten me through so many days over the last 2 years.

I was so taken aback from his outpouring of emotion and spirit. I had never heard someone openly question God so much, but at the same time really search for answers. "Mr. Morris, I am so sorry for the loss of Daniel, but I am glad you told me how you think about it and how you really search for some meaning. I feel kinda silly because maybe I act in these sessions as if I am the only one who has been affected by suffering. And I am disappointed because I don't usually come up with any real answers regarding my suffering."

"Hope, don't ever feel silly about your thoughts regarding the suffering you have endured. There is no monopoly on pain in this world, but knowing our pain is unique is a healthy thought. Knowing we don't have all the answers is also the right path. Approaching any complicated or serious spiritual question with humility is the only way we will find some answers, or at least some peace. And humility is only present when we realize we don't have all of the answers, and are honest about how we feel."

Winter

Chapter 10: Just Get Over It

I really felt a deep desire to do something nice for Mr. Morris over the last week. I have been so used to wallowing in my own problems that I genuinely felt good about doing something nice for someone else. Plus, Mr. Morris opened up to me more than any other adult so far in my life. Not that I need people to open up, but I guess I trust people who I know feel deeply about pain as much as I do. "Mr. Morris, I hope I am not going way overboard by doing this, but I wrote you a couple of poems based on what we talked about in our last session…you know, Daniel passing away. I dunno if they are any good, but I just thought about it and they came to me."

"That is really thoughtful. Of course you can share them with me."

"Ok, here goes…"

The Brightest Star

Memories are like bright shining stars
That sparkle from the past
The pictures stay within your mind
And last, and last, and last.

They make you laugh and cry
As you look back far
Showering its radiance on you
That wonderful, shining star.

The Memory

Life is such a powerful thing
What can make it stop?
How can a heart so strong
Give one single beat so weak
And one day halt.
How can our loved ones
Whom we know so well
Give up in the process of living
And vanish from our lives
FOREVER AND EVER…
I know the answer of the secret of life
And death
There is no end, but Eternity
Which is more powerful than life,
Is the Memory.

I could see him smiling as I finished, and his eyes welled up with water. He was holding back a tear as he looked at me very proudly. I had such a feeling of happiness because I think I was able to do something nice for him.

"Hope, thank you so much. That was one of the nicest acts someone has done for me regarding Daniel's death. I mean it. They are such simple and powerful poems. You have a gift."

No one has ever really told me I have a gift. Maybe it is just because of my parents, but I often feel not good enough. And a gift goes so far beyond that. "Mr. Morris, if you don't mind me asking, cause maybe it will help with some of the hard times in my life, but how did you try to deal with Daniel's passing?"

He paused to collect his thoughts. That is a hard question to answer. I don't think there has ever been a point where I truly have felt as if I have "dealt with" his death. It is interesting, when I was a kid I was a part of a program called Awana. I don't know if you have heard of it, but it is run through churches where kids meet on a weeknight every week. There are games, singing, and workbooks to complete. I really liked it as did Daniel. We liked to hang out with other kids, compete in the sports and games, and were both pretty competitive when it came to studying as well. Most of these workbooks involved Bible verse memorization, and as soon as we were able to recite the verses without looking, our leader would check off that we had a section completed and could move on to the next section. And as we worked through the books, the verses got longer and harder to memorize. Daniel and I were so good at the memorization, though, that we would often finish a book in a couple of weeks, where most kids would take the whole year to get through it. We were able to move on to higher and higher level books. I still remember getting stuck on one verse though, which is Psalm 23. I don't know if you know it but it goes something like, "Yea, though I walk through the valley of the shadow of death, I will fear no evil. For You are with me. Your rod and Your staff, they comfort me. You prepare a table before me in the presence of my enemies. You anoint my head with oil. My cup runs over. Surely goodness and mercy shall follow me all the days of my life. And I will dwell in the house of the Lord forever." I guess I still remember most of it. I was so happy when I finally memorized this verse and it is such a well-known verse, so I felt really proud to be able to recite it on command.

I used to always think of that verse whenever I was in a difficult spot in life. It was as if there was a confidence attached to knowing *I* could fear no evil and *I* could walk through the valley of the shadow of death. I used to visualize myself in one of those old fables where the children are walking through the forest and confronting dangerous animals and people. It was such a cerebral sense of danger and I was overcoming it with the utmost confidence because somehow I was prepared.

When Daniel was getting sicker and eventually died, I realized how unable I was to confront hardship with a confidence and boldness. I did not believe with all my heart he was going to be healed, nor that this was God's plan and I should just accept it. I wanted to cower at times, but then let my anger run wild at other times. And Daniel just kept living every day with a sense of confidence that if his life were taken from him, maybe there was a greater purpose. He wasn't afraid to talk about death, but he didn't want to stop living.

I wasn't even able to tell him how much I truly loved him and what he meant to me. He was such a part of me and I didn't have the strength and fortitude to really tell him everything I had wanted to. He was dying and I could see it. And it wasn't like a car accident, where someone dies suddenly and loved ones regret not being able to say everything they wanted to say. He was right in front of me, spending hours with me on a daily basis for weeks and months before he died. I think the biggest regret I have is that I wanted to do these really cool things or really loving gestures on some days. It might be getting him his favorite meal, or talking about his favorite book, maybe compiling some old pictures for him to see, or possibly taking him to a ball game if his strength would allow it. But you know what, I was a coward. I thought if I did anything more unusual or over-the-top, I was admitting to myself that he was dying, there was no hope, and I had accepted his death. I just couldn't confront that. I couldn't confront the reality of the situation. I couldn't confront seeing a part of me die, and it was the better part. I couldn't stop it and wouldn't accept it. And because of that, I let him down. I had the strength to make his last months and weeks the happiest it could have been for him. I had the power to show him how much he meant to me and let him feel such a peace about our relationship, but I didn't do it. I could have promised to take care of his daughter and make sure she is raised the way he would have wanted, but I failed to tell him.

I failed miserably, and I am haunted by the fact that I did not confront the shadow of death with strength. I ran from it. I ran through the valley with my head down, fearing everything around me, and getting weaker and weaker. I had my moment of reality, and I was unprepared mentally for the opportunity to put any type of training into practice.

Hope, I have seen tragedy in your life and know how difficult it is to face reality. You have faced it admirably so far, with a sense of humor, a contemplative nature, and an ability to confront it and not run away from it. I want more than anything for you to just be a normal teenager and be able to be fun-loving, silly and even stupid at times. You have earned the right to have that attitude. And even the grades which first brought you into this office do not matter very much in the grand scheme of life. But I do want you to know that the pain and suffering brought to you by life has hopefully given you a sense of courage to confront the reality of this sometimes harsh world, and still do something positive when given the chance. I don't believe your spirit has been completely broken, and I hope you get the opportunity someday to use your strengthened spirit to do something which makes you proud.

If a broken bone heals correctly, the new fused bone is actually stronger than before it was broken. I hope that as your broken spirit heals from break after break, you let it heal stronger and one day are able to use it to make you joyful and fulfilled.

"I really appreciate you telling me all of these things, *I said*. You don't know how many times I cried alone at night, wondering why certain things have happened to me. And I go to school and try to fake happiness, but during certain times in my life it has been really hard. I am not sure what to do and how to act. Some of my friends or family members who know about my circumstances would always try to help me 'get over it.' It seems to be a phrase which comes up a lot, but I keep thinking that I can't get over it. And I am not sure what 'getting over it' even really means. Let me ask you, if you don't mind, how do you try to 'get over' the death of your brother?"

You are right to think that to "get over it" is really hard, if not impossible, *he stated*. I don't even think it is healthy to essentially "get over it." With that phrase there is a notion that we can move on from a part of our history, or try to forget it, or even erase it. I gather that we both know how hard that would be. My past will always be a part of me, no matter how great or painful. My brother was such a part of me and always will be. And even as the days go by, and the acute pain from his death does wear off a little bit, I will not erase him from me because I learned so much from him during life, and learned almost as much from him in his death. It forced me to confront life head on, to determine what kind of person I really am and what kind of life I should be living. Daniel left a footprint which can never be filled by me, but I know that by keeping his memory alive, I am reminded of what it means to focus on the important matters in life and shed those little annoyances which get in the way. Because every day I am living, however good, bad, monotonous, joyful, painful, is a day that he will never have.

Watching someone die of cancer makes you contemplate just what a day means. When we are busy with work, or party with friends, or sleep the day away, days seem short and a year can pass without much thought. To a cancer patient who is on a definite timeline and knows death is not too far off, every day means so much more. The days get longer, the activities seem more important, the birthdays and holidays might be the last. Sometimes no one mentions it, but everyone seems to understand this concept when hanging out with someone on borrowed time. I remember hanging out with Daniel and Grace in the months prior to Daniel's death. They were both night owls, as am I, and so we would stay up until 3 or 4 in the morning sometimes. I think it was our way of hanging on to each day because we didn't know how many we would have left with each other. It wasn't as if we were having the most profound conversations or acting serious. We would watch movies, or tell funny stories, or just play games while the TV was on in the background. Daniel seemed to get a second wind around midnight anyway, and regardless of how bad he felt during the day, it was as if his primetime kicked in and would feel good all night.

As he got sicker and sicker, he still loved to stay up late and hang out with Grace and sometimes me. And the movies we watched seemed to almost get dumber and dumber. Daniel had immersed himself in serious matters for his whole adult life, but as he knew the end was coming I think he just wanted to live each day to its fullest. Discussing death or watching serious movies didn't appeal to him because I think it provided no joy to him in the moment. Those items are reserved for someone who wants to challenge himself or contemplate what life really means. Daniel knew what life was about, and had come to a peaceful state-of-mind, so his mind was free to live each moment in the moment. Funny, stupid movies may not make the world a better place, or make us contemplate life, but they provide that minute to minute joy I think Daniel was looking for. When others have asked me what I did with Daniel shortly before he died, I often tell them that we watched just about the stupidest movie ever, but we couldn't stop laughing. We have the same laugh and we think the same things are funny, so it couldn't have been a better tribute to how he is and was as a person.

So there is no "getting over it." We take these thoughts and store them up, just like your poem actually. We use the fond memories to bring us joy, but don't shy away from the painful ones because it reminds us to appreciate life and strive for something greater. I am constantly reminded, though, about those long days and how each day meant something. I have tried to live that way the best I know how over the last two years. But even on the best days, when everything is going so well, a small thought, song, or smell, can trigger a painful memory and brings me down.

"I am so glad you said that because I am not sure what to do with my memories. Should I think about them, try my hardest to forget them, try to understand why all of these things happened, try to give my parents some credit and think that maybe they were doing the best they could? I dunno. How do you cope with it, the pain from memories?" *I inquired.*

I really don't know if I have a good answer for you. It's funny, after someone close to you dies, everyone wants to provide the perfect advice. Maybe they are trying to be profound or comforting, maybe they read about dying in a book or magazine and are following the advice in those publications. I had a few friends who even audibly tried to guess what stage of grief I was in and then talk to me about how to get to the next stage. I know they meant well. Most of the time they really wanted to help, but didn't know exactly how to express themselves. The best advice or words came from people who said, "I don't know what you are going through, and I don't know what to say, but I know it sucks." It is such a simple and honest answer that for me got right to the point. So I will say it to you, I can't possibly know what you are going through, and I don't have the right words to say, but I know it sucks.

Because how can I possibly know what you are feeling about a situation which is so different from mine? I never grew up in an environment like yours and although I have felt pain in my life, I have never felt the type of pain you have experienced. Mental and spiritual events are always subjective. No matter how close you are to a physical event which happens to another person, you will never be able to fully understand the mental and spiritual phenomenon which is occurring inside of them. If I can use this analogy, how would someone describe color to a blind person? Let's just assume that this blind person never had sight and so her whole world has always been dark. Maybe the color red would be described as hot, maybe white would be described as soft or the color yellow as warm. Even black may be described as what the blind person "sees" all the time. But what she "sees" is not black, because black only exists relative to something else, to some other color or light. And no matter how good someone is at describing color, the blind person would only be able to understand it in an abstract way, as a concept. There is no reality to it and there will never be. But imagine, if by some miracle, that blind person gains sight later in life. What would she think about colors then? No matter how realistic this concept may have been and how much her brain was able to understand it from an intellectual standpoint, her eyes, senses, heart, and spirit together can be the only way to truly experience color. Color becomes real only after she is able to see.

I cannot know how someone feels until I experience the events she experiences. I cannot know the depths of someone's heart or soul because she described to me a joyful or painful experience. I cannot understand whether someone's spirit is broken or alive unless I am able to truly be there with her in the moment and see what she sees and really feel what she feels. And even then, I am still an imitator if something similar happens to me, or an observer if I am physically close when something happens to her. I can never be one with her mind or spirit. The grand events in your life are your own, and those grand events will shape who you are, for better or worse.

"So how does this help with dealing with pain?" *I asked.*

Knowing that you have been through unique events and you are a unique person means that others cannot possibly understand everything about you. So I don't have the answer as to the best way for you to cope. I know from my own experience that I didn't shy away from internalizing the pain and making it my own. No matter what people felt was good for me, I had to really ponder and decide what I thought would be best to help me deal with my loss and pain. I developed a few consistent actions I hoped would help me on a daily basis. One was exercise, and specifically running. I had always been into playing sports and working out, but I realized that after Daniel's death, the only time I really felt any peace was during or after a strenuous run. Sometimes I felt angry, peaceful, happy, or sad, or all of the above during my runs. My emotions ran the gamut and I wasn't sure exactly how I would feel as I was running, but I do know that after I finished there was always a sense of peace and clarity. My thoughts were clearer and my emotions and thoughts felt as one.

I also developed a way to deal with triggers I knew would cause pain. If a sound, smell, social situation triggered a painful memory of Daniel, I would try to find a private area and just let myself cry. Afterwards I felt much better and was glad I did not try to push down the feeling or avoid the moment. For me, I believed that each difficult moment was a hurdle, and even though there is no finish line to grief, attempting to jump over each hurdle provided me with a little more positive reflection and comfort.

The hurdles that have been presented in your life are high and numerous, for such a young soul. I would encourage you to sit down and really contemplate what actions can help you attempt the hurdle when a trigger comes about or when you feel in despair. Maybe there are positive outlets in your life which can give your mind and spirit a break. Possibly there are little actions you can take whenever you feel the pain coming on and you are not sure what direction it will take you. And even though I have had a traumatic event in my life recently, no one but you can determine the absolute best way to cope with and confront those traumas. I can help you through and can give you pointers, but you will have to develop those coping skills as you confront more and more hurdles on the path to your mental and spiritual growth.

"I understand, *I stated*. I am really glad you know that you can't understand me completely. I wish someone could understand exactly what I am going through and have gone through. But I like the fact you don't try to act as if we are the same, because my whole life is essentially a showcase for not being the same as others."

Winter

Chapter 11: Money for Nothing

Once again, there is another man down in my life. General Lee went back to his home last weekend. I really thought he was going to stick around longer, but I know his family probably needs him. I wish my father would come back to us, even if he just moves near us or at least calls me on the phone. General Lee was really sweet to me so I am not mad at him, though. But it is hard to get my hopes up and believe there is eventually going to be some fatherly figure who actually sticks around. "Mr. Morris, I am kinda bummed out because General Lee took off and went back to his wife and family."

"I am sorry to hear that. I know you really liked him. How did it happen?"

"Well, at least he did a formal goodbye to me after he and my mother decided it wasn't going to work out. Maybe General Lee came to his senses and realized his old family needed him and it was the right thing to go back. I had a sense it was coming because of some of the discussions I overheard over the last few weeks. The one positive I can say is that he was always decent to me and my mother. This was one time where the circumstances were just not right for their relationship."

"How do you feel about this transition?" *he inquired.*

"It is hard because I am torn. I know General Lee should go back home and hopefully be a good father to his family, something I haven't had in a long time. But I really did like him and he was one of the best men in my life so far. He taught me a lot of cool things and paid attention to me, which was sorta a first. My mother is really concentrating on her businesses now as well. So maybe that played a part in their break-up. I know she becomes obsessed with work and making money, and maybe General Lee realized he wasn't going to be a big part of her life. I can definitely relate. I can see that look in my mother's eyes and I am just waiting for her to start saying 'time is money' every day. Once she goes down that road, forget it, because no one is valuable enough for her to miss out on the money."

"That's too bad. I hope she puts her business and money in perspective and prioritizes your relationship instead."

"Why did you quit your job and then come work here? Was it because you had a problem with focusing on money?" *I wondered.*

"After Daniel died, I had no desire to do what I was doing. Don't get me wrong, I loved what I did because it was exciting and I was good at it, but I can honestly say that my job didn't in any way, shape, or form make the world a better place. I guess someone could argue that economic systems need traders like me, but to me it is not a necessary element to the greater good. I took leave when he first passed away, and my bosses and co-workers expected me back at some point, but I just never went back. I went back to school so I could do something impactful in the world, just like Daniel. He was my example, and I think being here, or at least helping young people, is my true purpose."

"Sounds like the right reason for changing your career, *I said*. I was wondering, though, having been in an industry which primarily focuses on making money, what do you think about the Bible verse that says money is the root of all evil? I like the fact that my mother is trying to support us and I know it is hard to be a single mother again, but she appears obsessed with money."

Actually, that verse is probably the most misquoted verse there is, *he stated*. The actual language is, "For the love of money is the root of all evil." It is a verse which deals with what you focus on, love, desire, covet. For me, investing and trading was never really about the money. It was the competition I loved. Making quick decisions which can have large impacts, and beating others at determining what the best move is. All the money is made on the margins, the spreads on a daily basis, and then knowing when to throw down and make a big decision when the opportunity presents itself. The money for me was just a reward or tangible figure which showed how good I was in the competition. It was no different than scoring points in a basketball game or seeing how many strikeouts I could get as a pitcher. The people I worked with, who treated the money as secondary, lasted longer in the industry and actually enjoyed what they were doing. The ones focused solely on the money were usually miserable in the long run.

As an example, I had two main bosses at my trading firm. They had different styles and personalities, but I saw how each of them viewed money and the results from that view. They were both super wealthy, and probably made about the same amount of money based on their percentage ownership. One boss was super bright, brash and outlandish. He liked to party and liked to throw parties. Money to him was power and status, and the ability to have whatever he desired. He wore the nicest suits, would often party at the most expensive spots in the city, buy the younger traders drinks all night, have table service, and always had pretty girls around. He was married, but I doubt he was faithful much of the time. He had several expensive cars, including a red Ferrari. One of my co-workers told me about a night out where after they had a bunch of drinks, my boss offered him a ride home. My co-worker was wary to accept the ride because my boss was drunk, but he wanted to ride in his car and my boss insisted. My co-worker lived on the north side of the city, so my boss jumps onto Lake Shore Drive and just guns the engine of this Ferrari. It is about 11 o'clock on a weeknight so there isn't too much traffic. They start flying by cars, going over 100 mph in a 45 mph zone. A couple miles in, they see a cop car as they zoom by. The cop puts on his lights and chases after them. Instead of my boss slowing down, though, he guns the engine and starts driving even faster. He flies by a couple of exits until he sees that the cop car is pretty far back. He quickly takes the next exit. At the bottom of the exit, he flies through the stop sign and turns left until they are sitting directly under the underpass of Lake Shore Drive. They wait a minute or so. They see blue lights reflected on the trees and ground on the other side of the underpass and figure the cop sped by and never noticed they had exited the road. They wait 30 more seconds then start heading west through the neighborhoods in the direction of my co-worker's place. My boss was just trying to drive straight, but also flying through stop signs and red lights for about 10 minutes, figuring the cop had put out an apb on his car, and it is pretty hard to hide in a red Ferrari. He was able to drop my co-worker off at his place and get home without being arrested. I guess the cop never got the license plate, and this was before some cars had cameras like they do on the show *Cops*. He was never arrested, although I'm sure if that same cop saw a red Ferrari driving around town he knew it was the guy who got away.

This was just a small example, but I think it showed how money was a tool for power and excess with my boss. Eventually it caught up to him because he ended up going through a divorce a few years later, which must have become messy as it took a toll on him mentally. He started underperforming at work and the other higher-ups started questioning his trading decisions and his vision regarding the direction and finances of the firm. The partnership eventually voted him out, and he wasn't able to latch on anywhere else. I don't know if there was fraud involved, or just bad decision-making, but it looked as if word got out around town and he became untouchable to the other financial firms. I am not sure what he did after that. All I know is that I saw him a few years later at a department store in the city. He had put on some weight, had a scraggly beard, was wearing pretty plain and scrappy clothes, and just looked like a shadow of his former self. I thought about going over to talk to him, but I just turned and walked the other way.

On the other hand, my other boss is still at the firm. He is in more of a semi-retirement advisory role, but still working. He was always a really jovial guy, down-to-earth, someone who you would want at your barbecue. He was never really flashy and didn't want to talk about money or status. He was also super bright, and approached his job in an almost scientific, academic fashion. To him, numbers, data, variables, spreadsheets, reports, were exciting. It was like a puzzle or a chess game, always reading the board, the competition, the environment to help him make decisions. It was educational to see how he worked, because no matter how many hours any young trader worked, my boss knew more information. Nothing surprised him. He was also a slow and steady hand when it came to managing. He wasn't managing to get to the next quarter or year, he saw the ups and downs as just part of the long journey, and it was his job to steer the ship through the storms as much as it was through calm waters. He, of course, made a ton of money and gained a lot of wealth throughout his career, but it didn't appear to change who he was. He also became increasingly philanthropic over the years. He supposedly came from humble beginnings, and really valued education. So he started opening up private schools in some of the rougher neighborhoods in the city, where students were charged a small amount to attend or received free tuition. It was his answer to some of the terrible city schools which were in these neighborhoods. I am sure it costs tens of millions of dollars to keep these schools running and my boss is providing those funds.

In observing my two bosses, I developed a deeper understanding for money and desires in general. One boss had an insatiable attitude where money and power ruled his world. The other viewed money and power as an afterthought, and eventually something which could be used to better the world. One man destroyed, while the other uplifted.

"Thanks for sharing, Mr. Morris. Maybe I can talk to my mother and ask about her motivations regarding money. At least it will give me some additional perspective. I know that she needs to support me, but her ambitions seem to take over her life and push me out whenever I am in the way."

"Have you ever read the book *Yertle the Turtle* by Dr. Seuss?" *he asked.*

"No, I haven't."

"It was one of my favorite books as a kid, *he added*. The book is about Yertle the turtle, the leader, or king of the pond. He is not satisfied with being king of just his pond and desires more. So he commands the other turtles to stack themselves up so that he can climb on top of them and survey the land. The turtle on the bottom eventually gets tired and asks for a break. Yertle ignores him and commands more turtles to stack themselves so that he can get higher and see the areas he can rule. Upon surveying the area, he notices he is the highest thing in the land, which gives him a sense of pride. Day turns into night and Yertle notices that the moon is higher than him, so he commands more turtles to stack so he can get higher than the moon. Just then the bottom turtle burps and the movement causes the entire stack of turtles to topple, sending Yertle into the mud.

I know it's just a children's story, but I think it shows that when we have an insatiable attitude about anything in life, we end up in the mud. Especially if we sacrifice the love for others in order to satisfy our desires. Success, money, sex, drugs, fame, even obsessive hobbies can lead to our downfall and hurt the ones we love."

Narrator chimed in, "According to Dr. Seuss, *Yertle the Turtle* is about Hitler. Are you comparing Hope's mother to Hitler?"

"Of course not, *Mr. Morris stated*. I understand the political implications, but we are talking about the core idea that if we step on and hurt others in order to achieve our goals or fulfill our insatiable desires, then in the end it will lead to hurt and/or destruction."

"Thanks, Narrator, for another enlightening interruption. *Maybe Narrator should fall in the mud?* Actually, I could never see my parents reading the book to me if that is the core message. Or, they would rip out the last page, when the turtles fall down. Then if I asked them about the end, they would tell me that Yertle was so happy to be number one and on top of the world, because of all of his hard work and success."

"I am not sure how to respond to your comment actually," *Mr. Morris said*.

"I was joking a little bit of course, *I continued*. Although, if I had to think of it from a best of both worlds approach, obviously from Korean and American worlds, I would have to conclude that it is ok to have passions, goals, and ambition. It is ok to strive for something greater and to try to be the best. But when that achievement comes at the price of our love and compassion for one another, then it has gone too far. I have seen many Korean family members and friends who have achieved success, and are using their God-given talents to the fullest. Many are even using those talents to do great things in the world, like save children's lives. They may not have gotten there without sacrificing in other areas of their lives, or without their parents' pressure. But I also know there needs to be a limit to the pressure and ambition, and a balance has to be achieved, because I have also seen family and friends who have crumbled under the pressure from others or the weight of their own ambitions. And in many cases, including with my parents, I have seen how love and caring have often been replaced by ambition and desires.

In the case of my mother, it results in her focusing on business success and money. Now that General Lee is gone, there is no barrier, or distraction to her ambitions. I wish I was more of a distraction, and she felt the need to focus on me, but I fear it won't happen. And if she starts working crazy hours again, aside from sports and friends, I will be home alone most of the time, again."

"I hope not. I know how much that hurt you in the past," *Mr. Morris stated.*

"Oh, I almost forgot. I wrote a poem about General Lee if you want to hear it."

"Sure."

"Ok, here goes..."

Memorial to General Lee

You were a nice man, and you listened to me.
We ran off like criminals into the night
To a new land, where you became General Lee.
I thought you were the one to make everything
right,
But you lost the war, and are now Korean Dude
Number 3.

Winter

Chapter 12: Interpret Meaning?

I am busy in my free time this week trying to come up with some poetry to show at my next session. I am so happy Mr. Morris really liked the poems I showed him. Maybe I can be an artist someday. I think both my parents would be so angry. I am supposed to be a doctor, or scientist if not a doctor, or a CEO of a big company, something very concrete, which will make lots of money, and provide my children with a better future I guess. An artist, unless you are Picasso, is usually starving. I wouldn't mind living the Bohemian lifestyle, living in France, meeting some French dudes. I wonder if they would be cooler than Jimmy. Probably, since they would be all cultured and what not, and be romantic. I think my father would be happier as an artist, and he is probably living the Bohemian lifestyle anyway, he just doesn't know it. Maybe his father made him be something more concrete. I dunno. "Ok, Narrator, since you are probably looking over my shoulder anyway, do you want to hear my latest poem?"

"Sure."

"Ok, here goes..."

A Flower's Pride

I saw a flower growing
Just growing in a pond
And of this tiny creature
I grew so very fond.

A tiny fragile thing
With foolish pride so silly
And yet I grew to love her
This tiny water lilly.

It had pink petals reaching
Like bright rays from the sun
I would sit and admire her
Until the day was done.

Now and then I wondered
Why she didn't drift
And I was so intrigued
One day I brought a gift.

For her I bought a pot
So she could rest inside

She thought me so ridiculous
To pots she'd not abide.

"You foolish, foolish human!
Poor, unknowing child
Get away you silly boy
For I am strong and wild!"

"My roots are deep in water
I cannot be removed
I will live forever
And all this shall be proved."

Before she could feel pride
The wind came with a roar
And of that foolish flower
There is a trace no more.

"Beautiful poem, Hope. Can I take it to mean it is better to be humble and grounded, even by the help of others, than to do something ourselves and get hurt in the end? Would it also be about your mother and your fear of her focusing too much on money and her business?"

"Nope. It is about your mom, Narrator. The boy is you and your mom is the flower. She flies away because you are too annoying."

"What, that cannot be."

"Just kidding. Don't get all crazy on me momma's boy. I just don't want to talk about every poem I write."

"Well, sometimes I feel it is necessary for the audience to understand its meaning," *Narrator stated.*

"The cool part about poems and stories is that it is fun to find the meaning of a work, or even the hidden meanings, themes and metaphors. If the meaning is always spelled out for an audience it may take away from the value of interpretation. Also, because people may have different life experiences as well as views on an artistic piece, why not let them come up with their own interpretations?"

"Their own interpretations?" *he asked.*

"Think of a work of art like a painting. Many paintings have different meanings and are open to interpretation by the observer. Take the Mona Lisa. One person might see it as a representation of a strong and silent woman, where another person might see her as sad. No one knows. No one knows exactly what Leonardo Da Vinci was really thinking at the time he painted it."

"I do."

"You do?! How is that possible?" *I asked.*

"I once narrated a short story for his sister. I was able to be around Leonardo quite a bit and so I know what he was like."

"Really, ok, what was he like?"

"He was a nice guy for the most part, but he could be a little smelly," *he stated.*

"Smelly?"

"Yeah. He was very obsessive about his work at times and did not take enough baths as a result. Smelly. Sometimes bad breath. And occasionally he would be a little short with his sister."

"Right. Short with his sister, I see." *I said with a sarcastic astonishment.*

"His sister, *he continued,* would do so much for him, like prepare his lunch. But she would bring him the same items day after day and he would scold her. However, one day he decided to play around with his food in his inventor sort of way. He ended up slicing up the bread and putting the meats and cheeses in between, sometimes with some vegetables or greens. After that day he was more interested in the food his sister brought as he came up with different combinations to eat. He definitely treated her better from that point on."

"You basically just told me Leonardo Da Vinci invented the sandwich. That sounds ridiculous. I just don't believe it. Did he have names for these sandwichy inventions as well?"

"Yes, one of them was even his namesake, The Da Vinci."

"Uh huh. What did it have on it?"

"Well, of course it had Italian bread…and then…um…had some salami I believe, some prosciutto, some goat cheese…olives…red sauce…"

"You are just naming items you think come from Italy. You are so full of crap. And why would they call their bread 'Italian bread' when they are in Italy? It would just be 'bread' right?"

"No. Not true. Leonardo would always ask his sister for some Italian bread."

"You must be fake Italian as well, *I joked*. Do you even write these stories or memories down if you really do narrate for others? God only knows what you will say about me some day. Probably that I was six feet tall and invented the light bulb."

"There is still time for you to invent something, don't worry," *he said*.

"You don't even get it. This has nothing to do with inventions. Maybe instead of me seeing a counselor you should be the one. But instead of one made for angsty high schoolers, a counselor for crazy people."

"That is unfair. Also, crazy people don't like to be called crazy," *he stated defiantly*.

"If they know they are being called crazy and don't like to be called crazy, wouldn't that make them NOT crazy?"

"I suppose…maybe…I do not know." *He doesn't know*.

"Ok, we need to get out of this conversation death spiral. Please go back to your Narrator room, or space, or other dimension for the moment."

"I will oblige. Just do me a favor and look up Da Vinci and the sandwich, you will see."

"Sure, whatever."

Poetry time over for now.

Winter

Chapter 13: Campground Races

"Hope, I know we have covered some pretty heavy and painful topics. Why don't we see if we can come up with some happy memories from your childhood. Can you think of any offhand which would make you happy if you thought about them now?" *Mr. Morris asked.*

I know that despite all of my parents' problems, there were times when they seemed genuinely happy, or at least played those parts pretty well. We didn't know too many people in my neighborhood, and we weren't really part of a big Korean community, but every once in a while my parents met some other Koreans and we would go to dinner at their house. They were good times for many reasons. I generally didn't have many friends to play with in my area so it was fun to play with other kids. I also didn't have too many toys, so I loved to play with other kids' toys when we visited. And my parents looked the happiest when they were hanging out with other people. I don't know if they just liked to get out of the apartment, or were faking it, but the reason didn't matter to me at the time. They were getting along and it felt comfortable to be around them during those nights. Sometimes a few of their friends even knew how to play the piano, so both families would sit around the piano and sing hymns in Korean and English. During those moments, they were very surreal, but I felt as if I finally had the family I was longing for. Sometimes I didn't want the night to end because I was afraid this feeling would go away. On our way home, I would observe my parents just to see if they would continue their good spirits and whether there was some breakthrough which would cause them to act this way all the time. Sometimes I think those ideal moments caused them to relax and enjoy our family for a few days or even weeks. I used to pray that we would continue to see friends like these, with the hope that whatever rubbed off on my parents would continue.

"Ok. Any others?" *he inquired.*

There was a period during junior high where my mother really made an effort to be around and provide for me. Before she started her businesses she had a lot of time at home when I was in school. Previously, she didn't really cook much Korean food and definitely not American food, but for whatever reason she got it in her head that she was going to cook every day. She told me to invite friends over whenever I wanted, and that she would cook American food. I think she felt guilty because of all of our moves, and wanted to try to be a mother who was around for me. So she bought one of those giant Betty Crocker cookbooks and started cooking away during most afternoons. She would cook these elaborate meals, including dessert, right from the cookbook. They were really good. I don't know how healthy they were because most of the recipes were for pretty heavy food, but they were comforting. When I did invite friends over, they really enjoyed the meals as well. Sometimes they wanted to hang out with me after school and eat dinner with us because my mother did a better job of cooking than their parents. It wasn't until my mother asked what kind of food I had at my friends' houses did she finally realize she was going way above and beyond what these other American families were eating for dinner. I was almost hesitant to tell her because I knew she would come to this realization, and was hoping it would not diminish her new-found passion for cooking American Food. Each night was something new and special. And I could invite my friends over without having to wonder whether they would be surprised or grossed out by our selection of Korean food.

This experiment only lasted a few months, though, as my mother shut down her American cuisine cook-off as soon as she opened her retail jewelry store. At that point I knew, even though this was a new endeavor, our idyllic, albeit short family tradition was now over. For me, I guess I really appreciated the effort, but was sad cause nothing good ever appeared to last.

"That sounds like another good memory, *he stated*. However, even in the two memories you brought up there is a definite pattern. There is only the expectation of temporary happiness and joy. All moments of joy and happiness are temporary by their very nature, but it would be nice to string some of those moments together, and create a genuine trust that the status quo could be one of comfort and happiness. Does this make sense?"

"Yeah, it makes sense to me. I guess that is why I don't ever expect good times to come, and if they do, I am always waiting for them to end. It is an apprehension which will stick with me and I don't know if I will ever be able to shake it. I suppose I become guarded as well. If I don't get too happy about anything in my life, I won't be as disappointed when the happiness is pulled out from under my feet."

"I feel sorry for the fact that you are unable to enjoy something for enjoyment's sake. The best joys in life are ones which are pure, and we are free to really feel those moments without worry or anxiety. What about other fond memories which may not have involved your family?"

Yep, I definitely have some of those. After my mother had some more money and was so busy anyway, she generally sent me away to camp whenever I had a break from school. The summer camps were the best. At first I was a little afraid because I knew I wouldn't know anyone there, but it forced me to be social, and for whatever reason other kids treated me better than the kids in my schools. I think it was because we were all placed in these closed quarters day and night, and so it just made socialization that much easier. And because we were away from our home schools, everyone was essentially a new student, so making friends was hard for everyone. When the normal "cool" structures were taken away from the social environment, so many more kids just got along. The camps also limited how much we could communicate with our parents. We were allowed to write letters, and possibly a phone call once a week or sometimes once every two weeks.

For me, it was a way to get away from my home environment and grow up a little bit. It also took away some of the pressure of having to talk to my mother because the camp restricted the communication. It was a built-in excuse if I didn't communicate with her during this time, and I think she was ok with it as well. Sometimes I would really miss my mother after being away, so the camps helped our relationship. I don't know how much she missed me, but I know she didn't have to worry about whether I was more important than her business. As I mentioned before, one of the phrases she used to beat into my head was "time is money." She generally said that when she was late to pick me up from practice, school, or lessons. I often heard it when I would ask her why she worked so late, or why we didn't do anything out of the ordinary during the week or weekends. If she was gone for the whole weekend, I knew "time is money," and I cost her money.

"Hope, not to cut you off, but even when you started to describe a good time, it drifted back to the relationship with your mother and the disappointment it was during those times."

"You are right. Crap! I can't get away from it I guess. As far as the camps, I just felt a freedom to be myself, or even whoever I wanted to be. I met some pretty cool girls, and a few of these camps were co-ed. I was still pretty shy at this time in my life, but I started to figure out what it would be like to be around boys, talk to them, and make them laugh. I never did anything with those boys, you know what I mean, but it was so cool to think of a guy liking me and not thinking I was weird or whatever.

When I am older I definitely want to travel. My camp experiences showed me that being in a new environment can give me a new perspective. I think if I traveled, especially to other countries, I wouldn't be thought of as just the Asian girl in an all-white environment. I would be something more. Maybe it would be hard to define me. Would I be Korean, an American, would people think I am different and cool because I am a foreigner? And I could explore without having to wonder whether I am doing something wrong culturally, cause tourists are supposed to make mistakes, right?"

"Hope, that is a really positive attitude regarding new experiences and especially travelling. Home life, neighborhoods, and schools confine us and define us. I think you are right that in a new environment you can be whoever you want to be. Class, culture, race can hopefully be thrown out the window if you allow for it. If your family has the means, I would encourage you to seek out new environments and definitely travel. The world is full of so many different people, cultures, and races."

"Right on, *I blurted out*. Isn't it weird to think that Asians make up a few billion people in the world? We are dominant in terms of numbers, but in America, just a small minority. I think that is why when people talk about race in this country it seems as if most people are only referring to black and white, while us Asians get left out of the discussion."

"It is true that most of the race relations initiatives deal with black and white, and do tend to leave out other minority groups," *he said.*

"Yeah, I know. Being from one of the smaller minorities numbers-wise, I can tell you most people don't mind seeing us on the streets, in their schools, or a part of their neighborhoods, probably because our numbers are not high enough to have a real effect on the local culture. But racial prejudices and attitudes still have an effect on us, even if we don't have a strong voice or advocate in public."

"That's a valid point. I am sure as the number of Asians grow in this country, there will be a lot more attention paid to your communities.

"Yeah, I hope so, *I continued,* cause remember the L.A. riots which happened not too long ago? Plenty of newscasts never even mentioned the Korean community, even though many Korean businesses were looted or burned down. I also think many of them were targeted because other minority groups were jealous of the fact that Korean businesses had taken over certain areas of L.A. Once again, back to the minority competition.

Why can't we all just get along? Narrator knows what I'm talking about. He now buys into the idea that there is a minority competition going on in this country."

Narrator chimed in, "I would not necessarily say I 'buy' into your argument, but I understand your perspective."

"My perspective? You know I am going to point out again that you are a British white male, and if something doesn't directly affect you then you tend not to believe it truly exists."

"That is not true. There are minorities in Britain."

"Where? There are like 3. And British whites are all pale and pasty. They are actually extra white."

"Well, the sun is bad for the skin, for the most part, and there are lots of clouds on our island."

"Ok, ok, *Mr. Morris refereed.* I don't think we are going to solve the world's race relations by talking about the sun and skin problems for white people. I think we got a little sidetracked while talking about race."

"Actually, it is kinda on point, because I am going to Korea over Christmas break, *I said.* I have never been in the majority before. Maybe it will be nice to be in a place where people look just like me."

"Cool. Well, maybe you will be able to gain some perspective and feel comfortable being around so many other Koreans. Is your mother going with you?" *Mr. Morris usked.*

"Nope. She has to work at her retail store since Christmas is the busiest time of the year. I will be going with my older cousin. I really like her so it should be a good time."

Winter

Chapter 14: Are you Korean Korean?

"How was your Christmas break, Hope? I know you were going to visit relatives in Korea. How did it go?" *Mr. Morris inquired.*

It was nice. I went with my cousin who is a little bit older than me. We stayed with my mother's relatives for part of the trip and my father's relatives for the other part. Both families live in the Seoul area, so we didn't have to travel too far.

I was a little disappointed with how scrappy the country still is. My parents lived there for a short period of time after I was born, probably to save some money and ask for money from my grandparents. They told me how modern America was compared to Korea, but that was many years ago. I don't think they have been back since. I expected it to be more modern because everyone said how much it had improved since the Olympics were in Seoul in 1988. Even our tour guide for one of our day trips commented that the income levels in the country had doubled since the Olympics 5 years ago. I guess doubling is really good, I dunno. If this is doubly good, I wonder what it was like before the Olympics.

Seoul was pretty cool and had a lot of modern buildings. I never realized it was so close to the mountains. I guess I have never seen a city with mountains in the background. We took a drive up and down a winding road leading near one of the mountain peaks outside Seoul. I liked looking down on a beautiful lake nearby and feeling peaceful. That was a far cry from when we were in downtown Seoul. People are on the move, and push if you are in their way. I know we might have been walking around aimlessly some of the time, but I don't think my cousin and I have ever been pushed so much. I am hoping it was just rush hour on the sidewalks and if we go again it will be a little more relaxed.

Even though I look Korean, I knew people could tell I was not a homegrown Korean. It might have been our clothes, or our hairstyles, but they could somehow tell we were tourists. My cousin's Korean is so much better than mine, so she is almost able to pass for someone being from Korea. Although I spoke mostly Korean when I was younger, I know my Korean isn't that good. People there could tell right away I wasn't a predominant Korean speaker. It made me feel kinda weird being treated as a tourist even though I sometimes thought of myself as Korean first.

"What was it like to visit your relatives?" *he asked.*

When we were with my mother's side of the family, we stayed at my great aunt and uncle's house, which was on the outskirts of Seoul. When my great uncle picked us up from the airport, he commented about how nice their house was compared to other houses in the neighborhood. When we got there I thought the house was kinda small. The bedroom my cousin and I slept in was the size of an American bathroom. It was almost as if we had to sleep side by side just to fit. I began to appreciate the size of American homes, even though I have yet to live in one myself.

We felt kinda cooped up in the house because my great uncle said it was too dangerous to go out after dark. Too dangerous? We were from Chicago and had hung out in Detroit a bunch of times. How could it be too dangerous? I knew Korea might be a little dingy, but I never thought it would be dangerous. Maybe my great uncle was just one of those overprotective guys, especially since we were his visitors and he was in charge of us. The only problem with being confined to his house after dark was that he loved to listen to the Beach Boys all the time. I wasn't sure if he played it for us because it was the most American group in his eyes, or he really loved the music, but it was Beach Boys nonstop. How many songs do they have anyway? I figured my great uncle would run out of songs at some point, but that never happened. And how are they able to sing so high anyway? Did their manager come by and kick them in the crotch before they started performing? Listening to a bunch of guys singing in high pitched harmonies for hours became a form of torture.

"Why didn't you ask him to play something else while you were there? Maybe he thought you would really like it and did think it was ultra-American."

"Ultra-American? As if two teenage girls from America would listen to the Beach Boys. It was on a record player. Who listens to records? He is just an Oldy McOlderson I guess. Maybe he used to make out with my great aunt while playing Beach Boys records back in the day and wanted to reminisce, who knows. What is your favorite make out music Mr. Morris, Metallica?"

"Metallica? Only if I were on some heavy drugs, which of course I am not. But we are not going to go down that road, Hope. How about back to your trip. What did you do next?"

We stayed with my relatives on my father's side next. Going there felt like a relief cause we were finally able to get away from the Beach Boys. Who would have thought we would travel across the world and have to run from the Beach Boys. It was definitely weird to see my father's relatives and stay with them since I have only seen my father once in the last few years, and rarely hear from him. I am sure they are not even aware of that fact, but I was content not to tell them. I don't know why I protect my father in those instances. Maybe it is my upbringing and the thought of embarrassing or shaming the family, or maybe I really just hope that someday my father will come around and then I will be glad I never told anyone about his actions towards me. He actually called me while I was there, which was a surprise to me. I wasn't sure if this was just his way of keeping up appearances since he called when we were at his parents' house, or whether he really wanted to talk to me, but I am past the point of psychoanalyzing him. I don't want to turn all psychobabbly like you, anyway, Mr. Morris.

"Thanks. I will try not to be as psychobabbly, as you put it, from now on."

My father sounded so distant on the phone, though. He asked me what kinds of activities we were doing and whether we were having a good time. I guess he was just checking to see whether our trip was going smoothly. I felt so sad because he sounded so uncomfortable talking to me, his own daughter. It was as if we were distant relatives, or even strangers. I know he hadn't spoken to me in such a long time, but sometimes I hoped he would call me and act like he loves me so much, even if he doesn't get to see me. I guess it silly though, and too much to ask of him.

This was also the first time I met my father's parents, my grandparents. It felt so weird thinking of them as grandparents, though, because I rarely spoke with them growing up and only knew of them based on the stories I had heard. I didn't even recognize them when I first walked into their home since I had only seen them in old pictures. My grandmother was nice and polite. I couldn't really tell what her personality was like since she didn't have much to say. My grandfather was shorter and quieter than I expected. Maybe he was built up so much in my mind based on the stories my father told, but I thought he would have such a commanding presence. It appeared as if he was more scared to talk to me than I was to him. I did ask him what it was like to be a doctor and why he chose to be one. I think he was touched that I cared about him and wanted to know more about him.

He told me that he first decided to become a doctor because there were so many children who died at a young age in Korea and he really wanted to help children live longer. I could tell he was genuine and I thought he became a doctor for the right reason. He showed me a couple of the books he had written, which looked very professional and were made for prestigious medical schools in Korea. I asked him if I could have one of his books. He looked surprised, but then smiled and gave me one. I really can't read Korean, so I am bummed that I won't know what it says, but it was nice to have a memento of him. I admire him. I know doctors in Korea are prestigious and I know my grandfather has a respected title, but I think he did really want to help people and the prestige came later.

"What did you think after meeting your grandfather and talking with him? I know he is an important figure in your family."

I wasn't sure whether to get angry with my father or feel sorry for him after meeting my grandfather. Maybe my grandfather put a lot of pressure on my father to be like him, and so my father couldn't handle the pressure and decided to come to America. But my grandfather was pretty nice and didn't act as if class, money, and prestige mattered that much to him. Maybe he is too old to care at this point, I dunno. All I know is that from the moment I was able to understand words, my father wanted me to be a doctor, and to be a pediatrician, which is just like my grandfather. But my father never said it was to help children like my grandfather stated as his goal. It was because doctors were respected and made a lot of money. I guess my grandfather wasn't around too much to raise his children because he was always working at the hospital, but my guess is that he set a good example by showing his children the reason why a person does something. There has to be some passion and desire. It's great to get to the top of a profession and social class, but what does it matter if what you do on a daily basis is really boring or painful to endure.

If my father thought it was so great to be a doctor, why didn't he become one himself? Which is why I then started to feel sorry for him. Maybe he did want to be a doctor, but knew he couldn't live up to his father's reputation and would always be in his shadow. Or maybe he didn't want to become a doctor, but was too afraid to confront my grandfather about it, so he put pressure on me to become one. Maybe he just wanted to stay in an upper class and felt that upper class people have certain professions. Except for the fact that most professions take hard work and he wasn't willing to put in the hard work. Whatever the reasoning, it was hard for me to think of my father and grandfather in a similar way. I thought meeting my grandfather would provide me more clarity about my father, but it just made it more confusing to me.

I also felt more confused, at first, about my identity after spending time in Korea. Before going there, for some naïve reason, I thought I would fit right in. But all the Koreans knew right away that I was different from them and treated me like I was different. They were very polite to me, other than the pushing in downtown Seoul, but they definitely treated me like a foreigner. I realized that I am more than fifty percent American based on my trip. I do look like a Korean, but I feel like an American. And I respect America. Where else can we have big houses, big cities, clean streets, fast food restaurants, amusement parks, water parks, and so much land. We did go to an amusement park, a water park, and some American style restaurants (Pizza Hut and McDonald's) in Seoul. The weird thing is that everyone there treats those new things as a gift from God, and it apparently shows how modern they are. But most American cities and suburbs have all of those things, and we just take them for granted. I feel fortunate to live in America. I guess my trip was positive, then, because I feel more at home and appreciative of the country where I was born and live, even if I will always look a little different than the majority.

I wrote this poem during my trip…

Homesick

I look to my home so far away
Over the vast and endless sea
There I'll return, in a year and a day
If it still decides to welcome me.

These days, my ceiling has been the sky
I sail on a magnificent ship
I look lovingly as the waves flow by
Never has there been such a trip.

The days have been adventurous and fun
The sea, so mysterious and blue
I'm accepted by everyone
My best friends are on the crew.

Daily, though I look longingly to the West
Hoping to see my own land
My beloved country I would love best
To walk upon its sand.

I now think of myself as an American, and if not solely an American, then a Korean-American, but definitely not a Korean Korean.

Spring

Chapter 15: Be My Grasshopper

"I am feeling bummed out lately, Mr. Morris. Maybe it is because my mother is back to working non-stop, so I have more time by myself and end up overthinking, but I thought I would feel better as I start figuring things out in my life. I feel better knowing that I am more comfortable being a Korean American because I can adapt to the Korean community and American community. I have some cool white friends and some cool Korean friends now. I am going to church an am feeling that maybe God does care about be, despite my crazy life. I am not sure what will happen with Jimmy, I think about him a lot, but am not sure he cares about me. And I know General Lee is not going to be around, but I have gotten over that loss a little bit. So I think these are mature thoughts, more like an adult, but I feel like such a child sometimes." *Mr. Morris was visibly laughing a bit and smiling as I finished my last sentence.*

Hope, you are funny. You are a teenager so you have so much in front of you to experience. You will fail, you will succeed. So many things are also out of your control. The one aspect of life that is within your control is how much you grow and change. I like to use the metaphor of the grasshopper, the moth, and the butterfly. All of these insects go through changes during their life cycle, but the grasshopper only goes through an incomplete metamorphosis, in three stages. The more developed insects, such as the moth and butterfly, go through four stages of development, and therefore through a complete metamorphosis.

If you look at a typical moth we encounter, it is generally drab in color and there is nothing really beautiful about it. It tends to wreak havoc if it gets in your house, as it may eat food in your pantry, or chew through your clothes. Moths also multiply pretty fast so once you have a couple in your house you will inevitably have a bunch if you are unable to find them. They hide and reproduce until they create a colony in your cabinets or clothes drawers. Back in the day people used to put moth balls in the drawers of their dressers, and although they might have repelled the moths, it left their clothes smelling pretty bad.

The butterfly, on the other hand, is generally a beautiful creature with unique patterns and colors. People wait all spring to see the butterflies come out for just a short period of time. They fly from flower to flower and add to the aesthetics of a garden or flower bed. Butterflies generally do not sneak into people's houses and start chewing up their food or clothes. They do not appear to hurt others in any way, and exist only to provide beauty to those around them.

The grasshopper is in a transition. It is close to being a flying insect, but its wings can only allow it to jump from place to place. It is a beautiful creature when its wings are spread and it is flying across the grass, but looks rather common and dull when it is in its sitting form. It has not gone through a complete metamorphosis, so it cannot fly away to find greener pastures.

Narrator jumped in, "If I may interject, there are plenty of moth species which have beautiful colors, and may even be more beautiful than a butterfly."

"Thank you, Mr. Entomology, which is why I used words like 'typical' and 'generally' because I am talking about the moths and butterflies that most of us are used to," *Mr. Morris shot back.*

"Yeah, really Narrator, *I said*. This isn't science class anyway. I got what Mr. Morris is saying, and he is right that most of the butterflies I see are beautiful and the moths are drab. Narrator, you are like a moth, eating through a good story. Can we get back to what Mr. Morris was talking about?"

Mr. Morris continued. As I was saying, in terms of the grasshopper, moth, and butterfly, I think people fit into these categories. Some are grasshoppers. They are in transition because of age or maturity, and plenty just stay in this state their entire lives. They make the same mistakes over and over again, never grow past their immature or juvenile way of acting, shun responsibility, never become wiser, and do not contribute to the world in a really positive way. They have undergone an incomplete metamorphosis.

Then there are the moths. They have undergone a complete metamorphosis, but are not going to have a positive impact on their surroundings. They may have boring or drab lives, never really become anything special, and accept mediocrity. Or even worse, some may wreak havoc on those around them, chewing away at the lives of others by the decisions they make.

Finally, there are the butterflies. They have undergone a complete metamorphosis as well, but they will impact their surroundings in such a positive way. They achieve goals, act sacrificially, are giving in nature, encourage others, and bring joy and happiness to loved ones and strangers.

They will have such a powerful and positive influence on others, sometimes even in a short period of time.

Like many teenagers, I think you are a grasshopper and still undergoing a transition in your life. You can jump from place to place, but are still trying to figure out exactly who you are. There is always a path to have a complete metamorphosis, and the path you choose may determine what the end result will be, and what kind of impact you will have on your surroundings and the world. The great part is that you have time to go through this stage and so contemplating what you want to do with your life is part of the process. I also think reflecting on the past and contemplating the future is the only way to truly have a catharsis, and thereby a complete metamorphosis.

"Yeah, I would like to be a butterfly, but I guess I am ok with being a grasshopper right now. Can I be your grasshopper?" *I said goofily.*

"If it makes you feel any better, I guess it would be ok to think of it that way, since I am a counselor and you are a student in these sessions." *Mr. Morris was half smiling.*

"If you see me in the hall, can you call me Grasshopper?"

"Ah…no," *he said.*

"Why not? It will show how much progress we have made, and I can even explain the grasshopper concept to my friends, in a psychobabbly way."

"As soon as you tell your mother about our sessions I will consider calling you Grasshopper."

"You know that is not going to happen, *I said*. Nice try."

"If you would like, Hope, I can call you Grasshopper," *Narrator suggested.*

"Sorry Narrator, but I don't think I want to be your grasshopper, unless I want to learn how to say the wrong things at all the wrong times."

"Hey, I was trying to be nice."

"Sorry, you are right. I will think about it, Narrator."

"Just to get back on track and make one final point, *Mr. Morris interrupted*, you have come a long way and I see the development. Enjoy the transition and enjoy being a grasshopper for a while. Teenagers are supposed to be in transition as they question, ponder, and grow."

Spring

Chapter 16: Followers of Love

When I walked into Mr. Morris' office and sat down he could tell I was visibly upset and he knew I was ready to blurt something out.

"Something on your mind, Hope?"

I was shaking my head. "Stacy, my supposed friend, asked Jimmy to the underclassmen spring formal. I could literally kill her. She knows I really like him. What is she doing asking a guy out anyway, since that is supposed to be his job? And now I don't even know whether Jimmy said yes because he was being polite or afraid to say no, or whether he really likes her. Maybe he likes her, but doesn't like her like her. So what am I supposed to do? If I go with another guy, I will possibly hurt his feelings if he finds out I don't like him, and Jimmy might think I like the other guy and not give me the time of day. And if I go by myself I just look like a loser, especially if I go by myself and then try to hang around Jimmy all night. I want to kill Stacy! *I could see Mr. Morris trying to hold back laughter as he was listening to me and seeing me get more animated. I looked at him, almost embarrassed.* I know, I know, immature teenage girl stuff. I know it sounds silly, but I get so excited around Jimmy and I think about him when I am home and try to come up with something cool or funny I can say to him the next day. And I think it was working and he really liked me. Now I don't know and I feel like my life is over!"

Mr. Morris was visibly laughing at this point. "Your life is over?! Take it from me, that is so far from the truth. But I don't think it's bad for you to feel this way. Young love, or infatuation, whatever you would like to call it, is something completely natural, almost a rite of passage. The fact that you are acting like any other teenage girl is a sign that you are well-adjusted."

"Well-adjusted? Thanks, Mr. Morris, for taking my emotion and making it sound so academic, so psychobabbly."

"I'm sorry. You are right. Sometimes I have to take off my counselor hat and not overthink the moment."

"I know you think it's silly. I can't imagine you ever acting like this in high school."

"No, I had my moments," *he stated.*

"Really? Did you ever feel this way for a girl that it almost hurt your stomach when you weren't sure what was going to happen next?"

"Actually I did. I remember I had a big crush on a girl in one of my classes freshman year. I knew her outside of school too, because she was friends with one of my friends. So I would talk to her every once in a while, but never had the nerve to tell her that I liked her or to ask her out. I went to a big high school and there were many different wings and halls in the school. We even had a couple of buildings so it was possible we would have to walk outside to get to our next class. There were 10 minutes between classes, which sounds like a lot of time, but it all depended on where your next class was. Anyway, somehow I figured out what her schedule was and mapped out what building and hallways she would be walking through during each passing period. I would then change my route and would time it so I would pass by her in the hall at some point. Sometimes if she passed right by me I would look at her and say 'hi,' but other times I guess I just stared at her as she passed by. I did get that nervous feeling in my stomach and every day I would almost slap myself in the face knowing I was too afraid to act on my feelings. The sad part was that this was the closest I ever got to her. She started dating my friend at some point and I guess I just moved on. I don't think she ever knew the kind of crush I had on her."

"Wow, Mr. Morris, I never would have thought that about you. I don't know if that was romantic or creepy, though. I never would have pegged you as the creapster."

"Creapster? Wait a minute. Actually now that I think about it, it probably was kind of creepy. But at least I fit the right age category to act like that. Once you become an adult, if you were to follow someone around town or show up randomly where she hangs out you would definitely be viewed as creepy. But in all seriousness, first loves or first crushes are important, and I am not going to take away from what you are feeling. It is genuine and I know it will occupy your mind for a while. However, I just have to say that if this first love does not work out, or your friend steals him, rest assured there are plenty of guys out there for you. You will have so many opportunities, and some of them may even be off limits to your friends," *he said with a smile.*

Wow, Mr. Morris thinks there are plenty of guys out there for me and I will have plenty of opportunities! I wonder if we were in high school together whether we could date. Maybe he would be too tall or cool for me, but I bet he would think I was funny. Screw Jimmy, anyways, if he wants to date Stacy. Stacy probably just shoved her butt in his face when he was bending down to pick up a pencil or something. I wonder if she learned that from one of those nature shows...how to present yourself to the opposite sex, butt first. Ughhh, I can't stand her! Mr. Morris is way better than Jimmy. Hopefully I will meet someone like him someday. I bet I won't have to display my butt for him because he will be smarter and way more cultured than Jimmy. But I really like Jimmy. Why do I like him so much? Oh, he is going to get it. Instead of coming up with flirty ways to goof on him, I am going to really goof on him. Maybe if I embarrass him he will know that he hurt me.

"Um, hello. Hope...knock knock, anyone home?" *He was smiling at me.*

"Oh, yeah, sorry, one of those moments again. I guess I get lost in my thoughts from time to time."

"More like all the time," *Narrator piped up excitedly.*

"Ok, whatever. I thought you weren't able to read my thoughts?"

"I am not able to read your thoughts. But I can tell when you just stare off into the distance for what can be hours at a time."

"Whatever. Also, if you want to know what creepy is really like, you should take lessons from this guy. If he weren't restricted to my story he would probably follow people around and not tell them."

"Not so. I let you know as soon as I was a part of your story. I would never act the way you stated in your comment," *Narrator protested.*

"Ok, Creepy McCreeperson. I will keep that in mind. Maybe that will be your name from now on."

"You are not allowed to make up names for me."

"Why not?"

"Because it is inauthentic to the story. I cannot just make up a new name for you, and therefore I cannot be given a new name."

"Oh, too bad Creepy. Or maybe I will call you Mr. McCreeperson. Or maybe make you into a rapper…introducing MC Creepypants."

"Ok, Creepypants is way over the line. You cannot use creepy and pants in the same sentence and definitely not the same word. That makes me sound doubly creepy."

"So you admit you are creepy. You just don't want to be extra creepy?"

"Nope. I am not going to even dignify that with a response."

"Hey, can you two chill out for a moment? *Mr. Morris interrupted.* I am not sure what we learned other than teenage love is hard and maybe we covered creepiness. I think it is safe to say we can all walk that line at some point. Hope, do you feel better about the situation now?"

"Not really. But I will see how it plays out. I definitely don't want to talk to Stacy or Jimmy, for that matter. I will try to take your advice and not think about it too much. Although I am gonna try not to be creepy like you two," *I said with a huge smile.*

"Once again, I take issue," *Narrator whined.*

"Me too, *Mr. Morris said.* I don't want to be linked with MC Creepypants either. Come on." *He smiled and laughed.*

"Ha ha, very funny, gang up on me. Glad this topic is over."

Spring

Chapter 17: Let's Be Friends?

I know I am supposed to take Mr. Morris' advice about Stacy and Jimmy, but I just can't stop thinking about them and getting upset. I don't know what to do. Stacy already knows I like Jimmy so I can't just yell at her. And I am not going to tell Jimmy now. He was supposed to know that I like him, I think. Maybe he knows I like him, but maybe he doesn't know I "like him like him." Maybe I should just tell him, I dunno. In the meantime, it is back to some poetry to help calm me down. "Narrator, since you are Friend Number 1 now that Stacy is on the bad friend list, and Kelly is not around, do you want to hear some of my poetry?"

"Of course."

"Ok, here goes…"

Losing a Friend

There is nothing sadder than losing a friend
Knowing that to your sacred friendship, there must be an end
A person you've shared your life with, the good times and the bad
And with that friend are memories of the best times you've ever had
There's nothing which can erase the friend, from your heart and mind
Knowing when that person left, a part of you was left behind
You feel the lonely sadness, the heartache and pain
You know that you will never see her smiling face again
You do not understand! You cannot comprehend!
Because there is nothing sadder than losing a friend.

Friends

Often friends will leave us
Because they think we're "uncool"
Every now and then we're betrayed
Whether at home or at school
Friends will go behind our backs
Making us feel sad and down
And before we even know it

The result is all over town.
Then there are our perfect parents
In whom we all can trust
But let me remind you
Imperfection is a must
If you still think there is someone
Whose friendship is more true
Than Jesus Christ's just one question,
Did that friend die for you?

"Hope, those are really good poems. I gather you are still thinking about Stacy, and possibly Jimmy?" *Narrator inquired.*

"Yeah, I try not to, but I just drift back to them when I am alone. I know it is something I said you shouldn't do, and it is probably not even good for me to know, like in *Back to the Future*, but can you maybe do me a favor and tell me if Stacy and Jimmy get married? Ugh, wait don't tell me. No, I do want to know. Tell me please."

"Ok. Let us see here, *he paused*. Stacy and Jimmy do not get married. In fact, your friend Stacy is twice divorced with a couple of children before the age of 30. She appears to be out looking for men all of the time."

"What about Kelly?"

"Your friend Kelly lives a modest life with her husband and kids. They appear to be really happy. And no, her husband is not Jimmy."

"I feel sad now. That was not what I expected. I know I have my issues with Stacy at the moment, but she is such a strong and cool person. Why wouldn't she be able to have a decent relationship?"

"I am no expert, *he answered,* but maybe she chooses the wrong men. Maybe her strength, as you call it, is overwhelming. If I may be so impolite as to give my opinion, it could be that her behavior is a little bit extreme, and the mean between the extremes is actually the sweet spot in life."

"The mean between the extremes? Thank you, Dr. Freud. Anyway, what am I supposed to do with this information now? And what if I tell them? Won't that result in the butterfly effect?"

"The butterfly effect?" *he asked.*

"Yeah, as in a few small changes can have a dramatic effect on the world, and of course the future. I think the original idea was that the flap of a butterfly's wings could set off a series of weather events based on the ripple effect of the flapping wings. But it really became a metaphor for how one little change to the present can have a serious impact on future events. Once again, just like in *Back to the Future*. Knowing the future is dangerous, right?"

He spoke up, "I hope the makers of *Back to the Future* realize how much they misdirected a whole generation about the reality of how past, present, and future events really interact. I can, however, assure you that what you describe will not happen, this butterfly effect as you refer to."

"So you are saying that if a person back in the day knew about Hitler and killed him before he could kill millions of Jews and start World War II, where millions more died, then that would not have had a dramatic effect?"

"Oh, sure, *he stated*, if you are talking about Hitler, then yes. That would have been the largest butterfly effect in the history of mankind. In addition to saving millions of lives, it would have changed the direction of so many countries and generations to come."

"So why wouldn't the same apply to my friends. I mean, wouldn't the knowledge of the future change their futures and the futures of other people?"

"Well yes, *he answered*. But your friend Stacy would just marry and divorce a different set of guys, and your friend Kelly would either be with the person she is today, or another average, slightly overweight, jovial family man. Often a person's nature does not change with extra knowledge, just the circumstances surrounding some decisions. And your friends are no Hitlers, so their impact on their surroundings will be minimal no matter what."

"So my friends aren't important people? That is depressing."

"They are important to someone. They are average to the world," *he stated.*

"So average people don't have an effect on the world?"

"A little, but that is it."

"What about the movie *It's a Wonderful Life*? Isn't the whole point that he thought he was average, or even worthless, and the angel shows him that he had a great impact on those around him. Wouldn't subtle changes impact the world?" *I asked.*

"Yes, but he saved his brother from drowning, saved his old boss from going to jail, saved a friend from being poor and possibly going to jail, saved his business partner from going to jail, saved people from living in poverty, and his wife was very good looking too, and he saved her from becoming not-so-good-looking. If your friends become lifeguards and save some lives, prevent many people from going to jail, give people funds for their houses to prevent poverty, and make their husbands better looking, then yes, they will have that kind of impact."

"You are ridiculous. What about me? I am average."

"Forgive me, Hope, for saying this, but you are not average. I can see your potential and understand why Mr. Morris cares about who you become. Your friends do not question their thoughts and motives in order to challenge themselves to become better people. They are content. There is nothing wrong with being content, but I do not think you are content with having a small ripple effect. Using your original example, my guess is that you can have a larger butterfly effect if you would like to."

"So you can see my future?"

"No, but I can see something more in you. Even the fact that you give me such a hard time tells me something about you. Most people I have narrated for just accept what I tell them and present to them. You want something more from me and obviously are not afraid to say so. And I see that you approach your life in the same way. You have had many hardships, but refuse to accept your lot in life and choose to seek out something better."

"Ohhhh, thank you, Narrator. That was really sweet. Maybe we can be friends after all. And I really only want you to get better too. How about if we get better together?"

"Agreed."

Take that Jimmy. Even Narrator thinks highly of me.

Spring

Chapter 18: Care to Dance?

I decided to see if Joseph would go to the underclassmen spring formal with me. If you remember, he is the Korean guy from my church youth group and I think he has a crush on me. He was really excited when I asked him to go. I wish that a boy would've ask me instead, but at least in Joseph's case, I had to ask him since he goes to another high school. I went with Stacy, Jimmy, Kelly, and her guy, and of course Joseph. Kelly's parents drove us all to a restaurant, since they have a giant van for their family. Kelly's parents ate dinner across the restaurant and we all sat at a table by ourselves. It was nice to be by ourselves, all dressed up, like real adults. Although the real adults in the restaurant kept staring at us as they walked by our table. It was probably because the restaurant wasn't too fancy and we were the only ones really dressed up. Oh well.

Kelly's parents took us to the dance after dinner, if you can call the formal a dance. It is a Christian school so they really monitor the dancing part. It is ok to dance in a group, but there are no slow dances and the guys and girls are not allowed to dance with each other alone. And definitely no making out. They play mostly Christian music, and a few other groups considered not scandalous I guess, like U2. I didn't mind too much since I like to dance to just about anything. Stacy and Kelly do too, so it was back to the 3 amigos again. None of the boys really knew how to dance, so they kinda just stood around us and moved from side to side a little bit. I am guessing they would be able to dance if they really tried, but maybe they were embarrassed. Maybe it is not "manly" to dance. I was really struggling to not get mad at Stacy though, since she was so flirtatious with Jimmy right in front of me. It was like a competition in her mind I guess. Whatever. Joseph and I were having a good time and I could tell he liked hanging out with me and my friends. He even tried to dance a little bit with my encouragement. Joseph has a really good smile and wasn't afraid to smile at me when I looked his way. Jimmy was smiling at me too when I was dancing, but I was like, "Whatever, dude, you are Stacy's now." The dance was fun, though.

Kelly's parents picked us up from the dance and even took us all out to Stake N' Shake for some shakes and fries. It was cool to just relax, laugh, and have a good time. When I was looking around the table and saw how much fun we were all having, I almost completely forgot about the love triangle, or supposed love triangle in my mind, between Stacy, me, and Jimmy. I was just glad to have a bunch of friends and have a good time. I would rather have a group of friends than fight over a boy. And who does Jimmy think he is anyway, God's gift to women? Come on. Joseph was really sweet too. I could tell his parents taught him manners because he would open the door for me and pull out the chair for me. Koreans are very strict about manners from what I know, and I appreciated those touches because they made me feel more comfortable. After we were done with our shakes and food, Kelly's parents took each one of us home. They are such good people, since they had to drive all over the place just to get us all home. At least this meant that Stacy and Jimmy weren't alone together since they were dropped off separately. Stacy wasn't able to use her girl magic on him.

Kelly called me the next day and told me that Jimmy told her that he had originally intended to ask me to the dance, but then Stacy asked him and he wasn't sure what he should do, so he just said yes. He told Kelly he thinks I am cute, funny, smart, and exotic looking. In the past I wouldn't know what to think about being called exotic, but I am going to take it as a compliment. I mean, who wouldn't want a boy to see you as exotic, right? So I guess Jimmy really did like me, and I wasn't making things up in my head. It is weird, though, because now I am not sure what to do. I really liked spending time with Joseph, so maybe I am not a one-man kind of woman.

Which is actually kinda silly. I know I talk a lot about making out, but I have never even kissed a guy before. I am sure it would feel good, but I am not sure I know what to do. Maybe if I practiced I would feel more confident if I am ever close enough to kiss a guy. But how do I practice? I have seen people kiss their dogs, but we don't even have a dog, and that is just gross. Some of the other girls in school told me that sometimes they practice using their hand. I don't even know what that means and can't even picture it in my head. Oh well. My only hope is that I am a natural, right? Even Stacy admitted she hasn't kissed a guy yet, which is surprising to me. Maybe they only kiss her butt when she sticks it out in their presence. I dunno.

All I know is that I really liked going out with guys in our group and having a good time. Maybe I am not ready for Romeo yet, which is a good thing. Plus, who doesn't like to have multiple options, especially from two different worlds, who may never know about each other, ha ha. Cool it Narrator, cause I know what you want to say, but you know I am only kidding.

So right now, I just like thinking about love and affection. Who knows what will happen. I will just wait for the right guy, who also wants to make out with me. Romeo and Juliet can wait.

Spring

Chapter 19: Here We Go Again

Mr. Morris could see that look in my eyes as soon as I sat down, so he knew I had to get some words out quickly before I exploded."Mr. Morris, I can't believe this is all happening again. You will not believe it, or maybe you will, but my mother has just gotten married again. Once again, I don't even think I have met the guy. Where does my mother find the time to do all of this dating, if she does? I dunno, maybe she is part of some mail-order program. Or maybe instead of a group of men standing in some parking lot because they are day laborers, there are actually a group of Korean men waiting to be picked up for marriage. Maybe my mother just drives by, picks out the one she likes, and tells him to jump in the back of her truck. Maybe there is a Korean man shelter where they all hang out in their own rooms. My mother walks in, observes their behavior, picks the one she wants, fills out the paperwork, and gets to take him home. All she needs to do is agree to feed him, clothe him, and bathe him occasionally."

Mr. Morris was holding back a laugh. "Ok. I know you are really upset, as I would be if this were happening to me. Do you at least have some specifics on the situation and their relationship? What is this guy like? Is he nice? Did they tell you how they met or their backstory?"

"He seems really nice actually. But I am not going to fall for that again. In my mind he is Korean Dude Number 4 until further notice. Maybe I should even call him that in front of my mother. Do you think she would like that? *I'm not even sure I am being sarcastic.* I can't believe it. And I thought my mother and I were past the whole, 'I keep things from you for your own benefit.' How is this for my own benefit? All these secrets and craziness. Because we were on spring break I didn't know what to do and just could not control my emotions. So I locked myself in my room for a couple of days and just wrote. Here are a couple of the poems I wrote." *I wish Mr. Morris could see my notebook where I really say what I think and has all kinds of instances where I call my mother insane. I think it would look like the ravings of a lunatic though. Maybe he would have me committed or something.*

Wishing

I thought I'd climb a mountain
Until I touched the sky
But I saw its foolishness
After years went by.

Then I thought I'd sail a ship
Across the sea so blue
I wished and washed with all my heart
My wish did not come true.

And now I wish, that if I died
God, my life would save
But my guess is that I'll end up
Wishing in my grave.

I Must Go Where No One Else

I must go where no one else
Has ever gone before
To secret lands and hidden coves
Upon the distant shore
Where gulls soar free
Upon the breeze
And horses run untamed
Where wild animals freely roam
Exotic and unnamed.

I must go where no one else

Has ever gone before
To have my peace and
Be burdened by all
Worries no more.
I'll build my home upon the sand
The birds' song in my ear
No sadness and just joy and life
With nothing left to fear.

Going Nowhere Fast

Here I am, living in the past
Thriving on memories and moments
Defined not to last.
Drawing out one second to the
Very End of Time
Weak from lack of sustenance
The chosen death, sublime.
This fate two-faced, unrecognized
Shrouded with momentary bliss
Reminisce of better times
The momentary kiss.
Staring at a blank brick wall
Alive with indivisible hues
Dancing with my mind's images
Whispered from my Muse.
Oblivious of what's To Be
I'm living in the past
Alone in my reality
Going nowhere fast.

Loneliness

Loneliness is a deserted world
A vast wave of emptiness unfurled
Vulnerable in a void so dark
Where arrows of sorrow hit their mark
In the depths of grief and gloom
Trapped in a suffocating room
A stab of longing in the heart
A gap that keeps people apart.

"Hope, those are really well-thought-out, profound poems, with imagery that really captures your emotions. Do you want to talk about them, or just let them be?"

"I think they are kinda self-explanatory. I wish God would grant my wishes and He doesn't, so I need to get the heck outta here, but I can't cause I am stuck, and so I feel like crap because I am lonely in my world. Geez, I can't believe all of this keeps happening to me the same way. Maybe after I write a poem I should crumple it up and then shove it down my mother's throat. Do you think she would be able to read my emotions then?"

"Ok, ok. I know you are getting all wound up about this. Forgive me, because I am not trying to diminish your hurt and anger, and am definitely on your side, but is there anything positive which could come out of this situation?"

"On the surface there are some things which look positive. He does appear to be a nice guy, and he has two daughters who are a little bit younger than me, and I believe they will be living with us. Maybe I will get along with them and have someone to hang out with in addition to my friends. And because of his daughters and me, I think my mother and Korean Dude Number 4 are going to buy a house in the neighborhood. I have never lived in a house so I think that is a really cool thing. And I am not sure if he just said this because he could tell I was upset, or he really meant it, but he said we could get a dog. I've always wanted a dog so that would be so cool if it happened. So yeah, I guess those are some positives."

"Ok, so why are you really upset? What are the core reasons?"

"Well, I have seen this before. My father, well, he is my father. He didn't provide much of a life for us, took off, and I don't know if he is ever coming back. Korean Dude Number 2 took us out of poverty and gave us a decent life until my mother decided it wasn't for her. And he started out nice and then became a jerk. Korean Dude Number 3 was going to be the next one to make our lives better, but he made a mistake and had to leave once he finally realized it. So what is going to happen with Korean Dude Number 4? Maybe he will stick around and maybe we will have some sort of family with a house, sisters, and a dog. Or maybe he or my mother will run for the hills once things start to go bad."

"Ok, I totally understand where you are coming from, *he said*. The pattern of behavior and hurt is something you can't, and shouldn't, get over until they prove themselves to you. Is there anything else which is making you upset?"

"Yeah, it is the way my mother went about all of this. Once again, she kept me in the dark for whatever reason. Look, I get that if she were going to date, she might only want to introduce a guy to me when they are really serious because she would not want constant attachments and then possible break-ups where my attachments to men would have to be broken. But waiting until after she is married?!! That is just crazy. Who does that? And even if she thought it was ok in the past, we have had these discussions and she knows how upset it makes me and how much it hurts me."

"I understand everything you are saying. She essentially broke your trust."

"Absolutely! *I said*. I don't have a lot of trust left, and as soon as I feel at ease and am able to trust again, the same pattern takes over and I feel the same way as many times before."

"I think it is ok, then, not to trust in your mother and the situation until they prove to you it will be positive, *he stated*. Definitely take some time to think about your hurt, write poetry, and let yourself feel bad. But I hope you get a chance to focus on some of the positives which have occurred over the year so far. You have been doing better in school, met some friends who care about you, have friends at this mostly white school, have friends in the Korean community, go to church and are trying to trust in the Lord, found your identity a little bit better by understanding the two worlds you have to navigate, and if I may sound psychobabbly for the moment, appear to be a well-adjusted, normal teenager. Although I have only counseled a small number of people in my time here, I can say that what has happened to you in life has been far worse than others I have counseled, but you also have the most potential compared to others. I believe your inner strength will continue to get you through the hard times, and propel you to being a light in a sometimes dark world. And who better to light the world than someone who has seen the darkness. I believe in you, and I hope you believe in yourself."

I wanted to cry, or smile, or shout. Maybe Mr. Morris was just giving me a pep talk, but I do believe knowing he believes in me. "Thank you, Mr. Morris. You are so kind and inspirational, and psychobabbly too, of course."

Spring

Chapter 20: Covet Hope?

"Hope, one question I always wanted to ask you during these sessions is why you refer to your parents as mother and father. Is that out of respect for them, or is it a Korean thing?"

"No, Mr. Morris, it is not a Korean thing, at least not for me. I have had Korean friends who were very formal with their parents, but for me it is a matter of familiarity. When I hear other kids call their parents 'mom' and 'dad', it sounds like they are really close. There is no barrier between them, and it is almost as if they are friends, or at least really friendly with each other. I don't feel that familiarity with my parents for the most part, so it is hard to refer to them as 'mom' and 'dad' right now. I hope it changes in the future. It is weird, because they have to earn my respect for me to use 'mom and dad.' In my culture, and many other cultures, it is definitely the reverse. I guess I desire for them to show me how much they love and care about me, and then I will be more at ease and reflect that with my speech. They will be mom and dad at that point."

"That is an interesting answer, *he stated*. I understand where you are coming from based on the familiarity aspect. I hope it changes in the future as well. Seeing how it is one of the last sessions of the year, I was wondering if you had any topics you would like to discuss. I know I have directed our discussions most of the time, but there may be something which is really on your mind."

"I guess I would like to know if you think it is possible for my parents to ever truly change. I know I have prayed a bunch, and we have talked about it in our previous sessions, but what do you think it would take for them to change, or anyone to change for that matter."

Mr. Morris thought for a moment. "That is a hard question to answer. I think you have to really get to the core of people to understand them and see if they really have the ability to change. If we can break down someone's deepest desires into a simple concept, we may be able to get at that core. The question is, what do we covet? Let's strip away the connotation regarding the word, and instead focus on its simple meaning. It is a deep desire that goes to the core of a person. It could explain the motivation for someone who helps the poor, or someone who becomes addicted to drugs. Find out what someone covets, and you start to understand his nature. Hope, what do you think your father covets?"

"I dunno exactly. I know he likes respect, and he always wanted to be thought of as smart and successful. He likes to think he is in a higher social class than others and his family is better than others. I guess it is a sort of pride, but it goes much deeper than himself and any of his own attributes and accomplishments. He wants people to treat him a certain way because of who he is, who his parents are, what his past education was like, rather than what he is currently doing and who he is today."

"Ok, let's think of a word or phrase which really boils down what you just told me. Would 'admiration' fit into that definition?" *he inquired*.

"I think so. That sounds like a good word to describe what he really wants."

"Ok, so he covets admiration. Now let's turn to your mother. What are some of her desires?"

"I know she is competitive, wants people to really notice her, hopes others will recognize her talent, can often be the center of attention, and can be very focused on her own goals and life. Sometimes I think it is very inward, like an inner drive, but I often find myself thinking that all she does, including her own inner goals, is so people will praise her."

"Based on what you just stated, would 'adulation' be a good word to describe her desires?" *he asked.*

"Adulation. Hmm, I do think it fits with what she really desires."

"Ok, your father covets admiration and your mother covets adulation. I am of the belief that what we covet determines our nature, and our nature determines our actions. So your father and mother will do things in this world to seek out that which they covet. If they do not feel fulfilled by another person, their family, or job, then they will change their circumstances to quench their desires. Or they will be on a constant journey, never satisfied because their covetous desires may be unrealistic.

Take your father, for instance, do you give him admiration, and even if you don't outwardly give it, does he feel admiration from you?"

"I want to admire my father and I always hope he becomes happy and then spends more time with me. But I don't really respect him, and so I guess I don't admire him at this time."

"What about your mother? Do you give her adulation?"

"No. I sometimes compliment her on the fact that she is a successful businesswoman, and can be loving and thoughtful at times, but I know I don't give her adulation. If anything, I am a reminder of some of the mistakes she has made because I know her deep secrets. I am probably preventing her, at least in her mind, from being free to achieve her goals, which will then bring her adulation."

"Ok, so your parents covet admiration and adulation, *he continued*. You are not able to provide those for them. In turn, they must look to the world, but the world may or may not fulfill those desires. If they are fulfilled by the outside world, then they may not have to look to you for fulfillment. But then it will probably go one of two ways. Either they are able to have a comfortable relationship with you because there is less pressure on you to be something for them which you are not. Or, they will ignore you to seek out more and more fulfillment from the outside world.

If, however, they are unfulfilled by the outside world, then they will probably be angry and direct that anger at any person or entity they believe is responsible for their unfulfillment. In that case, they may perceive you as responsible for their unfulfilled desires."

"That makes a lot of sense actually, *I stated*. I think my mother ignores me because other people praise her way more than me. She is the boss at work, so I am sure her workers give her compliments or praise. There have obviously been Korean dudes who seem to give her a lot of attention. I tell her I love her, but I can't give her the praise she desires. Maybe my wounds are too deep, or my mother keeps hurting me in the same way, but I really know I can't give her what she wants.

My father, on the other hand, wants admiration, but I don't think he is going to get any. Maybe if he went back to Korea and worked alongside my grandfather he may get some of the admiration he seeks. In America, we value hard work and success. I don't know if he is ever going to achieve a high level of success, and so he is not going to get much admiration from the outside world. But many fathers can get admiration from their children by just loving them and being there for them. I wish my father could do that, and he would get my admiration. I never cared whether he was successful or not. All I ever wanted from him was his love. It is funny, because whenever I try to do something really well, I always think of my father first. Maybe it is unrequited love, or maybe I am chasing a ghost, but I really desire to please my father. It could also be because I am so much more like him, and so I want to be close to him."

"I feel really bad for you, Hope. I wish your father would turn his life around and come back into yours. I also wish your mother would be fulfilled in some way, so she could focus more on you. I do think, though, it is good to be cognizant of the fact that what they covet is driving their decisions. And unless they have an inner transformation, I don't think their behavior will be altered substantially."

"I know. I really do. I have prayed and cried out to the Lord for my parents' hearts to change so many times. Or sometimes I just hope they will find whatever they are looking for, so they can come home to me. My mother is part of the way there sometimes. I really feel it. I see that when she goes to church it does make her think about things in a deeper way. Sometimes she is more attentive to me and really focuses on the important things in life. But then I can see her behavior change over the next few days or weeks, as if she has an addiction to bad behavior. My father, though, I don't know if he is lost to me. I sometimes wonder what he thinks about or whether he thinks about me when I don't hear from him for months or years. I remember watching *A Christmas Carol* on TV and hoping my father would be visited by some spirits who help him change his heart, because I don't know how much more praying I can do. Or sometimes I would picture my father on a journey through land and sea, and once he reaches his destination, there would be a feeling of peace, and then he would be free to come home and be with me."

"There is always hope, Hope. I truly believe your parents can change, and I wish your prayers are answered. I really do."

“Mr. Morris, I know this is such a silly or complicated question, but why do you think God doesn’t answer our prayers?”

I wish I had the answer as to why some prayers are answered and others aren't. The right answer always seems to be that "God works in mysterious ways." But I think that is just a lazy phrase which simply means, "I don't have the answer." Maybe some of our prayers will never be answered, or maybe we just have to be patient. For centuries scholars have debated why prayers go unanswered, or why a good and perfect God allows evil in the world, as well as why bad things happen to good people. It is the idea of theodicy, or to put it more bluntly, the problem of evil. They are very complicated ideas which no one has been able to figure out. I know my prayers weren’t answered regarding Daniel, and He let a faithful, sacrificial, great man die of a horrible disease. I still don’t have the answer as to why tragic events are even allowed to occur in this world. I can tell you, though, that I am a better person today because of the sacrificial way Daniel chose to live his final months, weeks, and moments. I have hopefully carried on his legacy with the direction my life has now taken. I am not sure why God has let so much pain and destruction into your life, even as you cry out to him with every ounce of your being. I wish I had the perfect answer for you, but I don’t.

If I can say anything about tragedy and unanswered prayers, though, is that I have seen in others as well as in myself, a motivation to do something beyond what we had expected from ourselves before the tragic event occurred. Hopefully it makes us more compassionate, knowing there are others who have had pain and sadness. It may also show us that life is short and there may only be a few opportunities to really achieve our goals and positively impact those around us. I can imagine if my brother Daniel had waited until he was older to help others, he would have missed out on the joy of his calling, and the people he helped would have missed out on the blessings he provided.

Most of all, though, I think we should never lose faith and never lose hope. I don't believe there is such a thing as false hope. I heard that phrase a lot when I was dealing with Daniel and his cancer. I think hope is hope, and results are results. Whether the results are what we hoped for or not, the hope is what keeps us going and alive on a daily basis. Results are not what get us up in the morning, because they are in the past. Hope is what drives us forward. I often think of Romans 8:20, 24 when I am not sure why I pray or hope. "For I consider that the sufferings of the present time are not worth comparing with the glory that is to be revealed to us. For in this hope we were saved. Now hope that is seen is not hope. For who hopes for what he sees? But if we hope for what we do not see, we wait for it with patience."

Hopefully the glory in your life that will be revealed to you is worth all of the pain and suffering you have endured. I do know you have been thrown into the fire and I see you still have strength. After the fire, a blacksmith is able to shape the metal into something stronger and more powerful than what went in. You will be stronger because of what you have endured, I really believe it.

I have seen so many good, God-fearing people in this world. Many of them don't take too many chances in life, do the right thing, raise their kids right, and also focus on not doing the wrong things much of the time. Are they a credit to society, a positive on the scale of life? Yes. But how many of them have dug down deep, to use all of their energy for the greater good, or changed the direction of their lives because they have seen the depths of their souls? People in peril often have a chance to produce great outcomes in this world. A diamond is formed from thousands of years of pressure. A pearl is formed from irritation in an oyster which may be as small as a grain of sand. I am hoping the pain you have endured will somehow make you into a better person, and that person can walk out into the world and be really impactful.

Your name is Hope, and so it is only fitting that you continue to hope no matter what life brings your way. I sincerely pray that, although it may take patience on your part, you will have the opportunity to experience joy in your life and bring joy to others.

"Thank you for saying those uplifting thoughts, Mr. Morris. I will continue to pray and hope, hope and pray. You are so encouraging to me, and I really trust your wisdom and inspirational words. In regards to my father and what he desires or covets, I know I will probably never be enough to make him truly happy and fulfilled. So I don't know if he will ever come back into my life in any real way. I was thinking about that lately so I wrote a poem which has a little message of hope about him."

The Toy Boat

There was once a little girl
Who wished to sail at sea
She thought there was, at the edge of the earth
A place called Eternity.
So one day she set out a toy ship
It's fluttering sails bright green
Saying, "Come back sometime my ship
And tell of all you've seen."
She watched and watched the tiny boat

Until it sailed away
Hoping that her precious boat
Would then come back one day.
Months, years passed, in all about seventy
And now the young girl is an old woman,
The ship gone from memory.
She sat at the shore in her old hometown
Her happiness complete
When suddenly, the old woman moved
As something bumped her feet.
Scratched and scarred was her toy boat
Returned to her at last
Fulfilling the dreams of a little girl
From the distant past.

"That is a beautiful poem, Hope. I pray that no matter how long it takes, your father eventually comes back to you."

"Me too. Me too."

Spring

Chapter 21: Teenage Angst

My mother and Korean Dude Number 4 found a nice house in a nice neighborhood. I was so happy moving into a house. It has a yard, and a park not too far away where we can walk our dog. And yes, we got a dog, just as Korean Dude Number 4 had promised. He is looking better in my eyes based on keeping that promise. The house has a lot of space too, and I still have my own room, even though I will be living with my two stepsisters. They are a few years younger than me, and we get along so far. They treat me well too, in an old school Korean way of giving respect to your older siblings. It is cute, although I think they generally mean it. I don't necessarily think this is the family I always wanted, but I am willing to see how it goes. Hopefully there is no packing up the car and heading off into the night, by either group, anytime soon. Korean Dude Number 4 has continued to be a nice guy too. He is, of course, kinda old. I think he is older than my mother, but probably not as old as General Lee.

My mother has been working a lot lately, but at least I'm not coming home to an empty house. My stepsisters are usually home when I get there. I don't feel as inclined to turn the TV on, to be my friend, the way it used to be. I am still reading a lot, and have my own private space whenever I need it. Having a decent sized house is great, because when I want to socialize I can, but when I want to be alone I can always find another place to go. Right now, the relationship with my mother is on the upswing. I guess being apart a lot makes us enjoy the time we spend together, when we do get the chance. I think having other people around to act as a buffer, and smooth out any resentment which usually builds up between the two of us, is also a good thing. She can work long hours now, knowing that I am not left alone all of the time. And I value the fact that she has been making an effort to pay attention to me when she is around. Hopefully she is attempting to achieve some sort of balance in her life. Maybe it is because she is going to church more nowadays. And she is bringing Korean Dude Number 4, which is definitely a good sign. No more hiding, which is what I like to see.

I continue to go to youth group at our Korean church. I have been making some friends there, and I still like to see Joseph. He is such a sweet guy. I still do like the fact that the environment is different from what I am used to in school. I realized, too, that many of the people who attend the youth group are going through the same things I am. Most of them are in predominantly white public or private schools, so they are usually in the ultra-minority. And most of their parents are first generation immigrants from Korea as well. There is a bond between people in similar situations, even if it isn't always stated. But we definitely have gotten used to talking amongst ourselves about the struggle, even if it is mostly to describe things happening to us in a funny way. There is a comfort level, as well, in our willingness to open up. I am comfortable telling my white friends some of the struggles I have had with my family, but I noticed that some from my youth group really only like to tell the weird idiosyncrasies, embarrassing details, or secrets from their families to other Koreans. Maybe they trust that other Koreans will understand better, or maybe they believe we will know how to keep certain details amongst ourselves, especially if we think the information would bring shame on their families. Whatever the reason, I appreciate others opening up to me about their family dynamics and struggles. No one has been able to compete with my family's craziness just yet, but it makes me feel better to know I am not the only one who has family issues.

I have been hanging out with Stacy, Kelly, Jimmy, and Joseph a lot lately. And I have even been inviting some of my friends from Korean youth group to come and hang with us. It is the first time the groups from either side have hung out with other races this much. They all seem to get along, and even ask questions about their differences. I feel so confident by making my two worlds collide. Since I am really into 80s music, and the song fit, I even played INXS *Never Tear Us Apart* the other day when hanging out with the whole group.

No one thought of the whole two worlds colliding thing while it was playing, except for me. I know if Mr. Morris were here he would know exactly what I was doing. He would be so proud of me, his grasshopper, even if he wouldn't admit it and call me Grasshopper. What if I turn psychobabbly all the time, though? This is some dangerous interpretation going on in my head. I have to remember how to separate everything out from time to time and let my mind relax. Hmmm, maybe making out would help with that. I am surprised no one in the group is dating, and definitely not making out. I was hoping at least a couple of people would make out while we were hanging, so I can take notes. I dunno, is that creepy or cool?

"The creepiest," *Narrator weighed in.*

"Ugghh, I knew you were going to jump in on that one. Still doesn't rise to your creepiness. Narrator, based on your observations, who is the best looking girl in the group? Tell me why, and describe your thoughts in detail."

"Well, based on all of my careful and detailed observations about them—"

"See, that is creepy. Busted, Narrator. I just set you up. The correct answer from a non-creepy person would be that you haven't paid much attention, but if you had to come up with an answer…blah blah blah"

"Hey, I thought we had a breakthrough not too long ago and we were going to be nice to each other."

"You're right, Narrator, I am sorry. If it makes you feel any better I only joke around with you because I like you. If I didn't I would probably just ignore you."

"Thank you. I will take that into consideration."

I turned 15 recently, so I guess I am almost an adult, right? I dunno. I could see Mr. Morris shaking his head and laughing a little if I asked him that. Maybe being a teenager, and all the angst and changes which go with it, is ok. We have been watching a lot of 80s movies recently. *The Breakfast Club, 16 Candles, Ferris Bueller's Day Off*, and so many others. They definitely hit the spot with the teenage angst, and I thought they were cool since a lot of them were set in the Chicago area. It is strange, though, that most of the kids in the movies seemed to have so much angst from who knows where. Not that their lives can't have angst when they live in nice suburbs with relatively stable families, but their lives didn't seem that bad to me. It's all relative I guess. I can picture a hypothetical where I meet a character from one of those movies and she is complaining that her mother doesn't pay enough attention to her, or her boyfriend doesn't think she is cool enough, or she isn't rich enough to fit in with the rich kids. Woe is me! I would probably compete by saying that my father doesn't talk to me, my mother generally doesn't pay attention to me, I am dealing with a long list of Korean father figures, grew up poor, have always struggled with fitting in because I am always the new kid, and oh, yeah, that whole minority thing and looking different. She would probably feel better about her angst at that point.

Maybe the trick is to be around others who may have it worse than yourself, so your reality doesn't seem that bad. Maybe I should head to a homeless shelter and play the reality game with one of the teens. I could say that my father doesn't speak to me, maybe she would say that her father abandoned her or she never knew her father. I could say that my mother doesn't pay much attention to me. She could say that her mother is a drug addict, sees her off and on, and she has been in foster care for portions of her life. I grew up poor, but my mother has started to make some money. She grew up poor and has just gotten poorer. I don't have a boyfriend. Maybe she can't even go to one school long enough to be friends with a boy. I am a Korean struggling in an all-white town. Maybe she is black and experiences more racism than I do. I guess my angst would start to simmer down at that point.

But do I want to let my angst go, and is it misplaced? The whole method of getting out of a crappy situation is actually acknowledging the crappy situation, and longing for something better. Hopefully someday I, along with all of the other crappy-situation-dreamers, get a chance to break out. Because I think if you don't break out you become destitute, realizing that the reality of life is never going to change. Until I am old enough to break out, though, I guess I have to train my mind and keep my spirit strong. I wonder if that is why the black spirituals were so good. Brought about from years of heartache and anguish during slavery, their situation was not going to change, so they had to find some way to keep their spirits strong. Singing songs may have been the only thing which kept them going on a daily basis. Or how about blues music, turning sorrow into almost an ironic battle cry for life. I think a sense of humor is something which keeps people alive as well. Laughing at your own desperate situation has to make for some really cool jokes and a unique way of thinking. Maybe most comedians come from hard upbringings. I guess all of these things are cathartic. Kinda like mind over matter, the dualism of self, coping skills, determining my nature, psychobabbly blah blah blah. Maybe someday my life experience will be funny to me, or at least give me some deep perspective.

Spring

Chapter 22: The End of The Beginning

"Ok, Hope, this is the last session of the year. We have covered so much during the last year so it would be hard to recap or recount all of it. I also think it would be a disservice to your life to try and put what you have dealt with into some nice little box with a perfect slogan."

"Thank you for understanding, Mr. Morris. I don't know how I could possibly come up with a slogan or cliché anyway. I guess the popular statement for any believer to say would be, 'For every door that closes, one opens.' Or some say, 'For every door that closes, a window of opportunity opens.' So far my life has been more like, 'A door slams in my face over and over again and every once in a while I need to jump out the window.'" *He was smiling and laughing.*

"Don't ever lose your sense of humor, even if it is here just to get you through the hard times."

"One thing I was contemplating recently is my angst, *I said*. I know it is common amongst people my age, but sometimes I think I am silly for feeling this way so often. Do you think it is normal? Do you think my angst is misplaced on my part?"

I know this will be somewhat of a long answer, but when you used the word "normal" in your question, I thought about changing the word to "natural," and thus in our nature as humans.

In my view, what comes from God is natural. If Jesus was fully God and fully human at the same time, then it meant he had the thoughtful, emotional, and spiritual elements of human beings. Thus, he had elements of determinism and existentialism within his life and ultimate death. And determinism vs. existentialism is the very essence of our struggle, what actions are determined versus what actions are of our own free wills. Jesus was determined to die, but his existential human side did not want to die, thus he prayed and cried out hoping to escape pain and death. Jesus chose to die, and fulfill that which was determined for him. How we approach what has happened to us which is outside of our control is our own existential, free will determining our actions and future. Whether our paths lead to the right choices are in our hands.

Our minds fluctuate between determinism and existentialism all the time. There are events which are truly outside of our individual control, including war, certain diseases, some car accidents, and the list goes on. But so many of our actions and events are determined by our own free will. If our existence depended solely on the choices we made, our spirits would often be extremely depressed. I met many co-workers who had very determinist attitudes. They often didn't like their jobs, but showed up to work every day. They would complain that they "had to work this job." Usually it was determined in their minds because they bought a big house, had children, nice cars, or nice things, and thus needed that job. But who made those choices for them? Even though they were complaining, it probably made them feel better to "have to" go to their unfulfilling job day in and day out, rather than believe they were making a conscious, free-willed choice to show up every day. If most of our actions are free, then it would be mentally damaging to feel the weight of all of our choices, because they are full of mistakes, missteps, or just simply box us into a corner. The weight of our conscious minds knowing that all of our mistakes are our own can be crushing.

Teenagers are in a different and awkward position where many of their decisions are made by their parents. It could be freeing to know the weight of any mistakes is not placed solely on their shoulders, and therefore their conscious minds, but generally it is burdensome to know their free wills are stymied. How teenagers view and feel about some of the choices outside of their control is the only purely existential part of themselves at times, which is a difficult position to be in. They really are subjected to determinism, but at a time in their lives when they truly desire existential choices.

So, by nature, angst is simply a reflection of the determinist/existential scale weighted against us, at least in our minds, with it being weighted more unfavorably towards teenagers. Their spirits cry out for freedoms in an environment ruled by predetermined choices. Thus, teenage angst, however big or small, is never really misplaced. The only question is whether the response is equal to the agitation, and how a teenager views and acts on that built-in angst.

I believe you have every right to have angst, Hope, and your level of angst is definitely not misplaced based on what you have been through in your life. Many of the choices in your life have been made for you, and many of them have been bad choices. I am sure you have desired to make your own choices when you see the mistakes the adults in your life are making. So the determined actions have hurt you, and you have no freedom to overcome those actions.

I do see, though, that you have used whatever freedom you do have to attempt to work through your life's struggles in an effort to become a great person. I am proud of you. I know it might not be a word you hear a lot, but I can see how hard you have worked to become who you are today. But the journey is not over, and you have your whole life ahead of you. And at some point, your life will be your own, and you will be able to create your own path.

"Thank you for saying such nice and sweet things, *I said*. I am glad my angst is not too crazy. It makes me feel good to know I am normal, at least when it comes to that part of my life. You are right, I haven't heard the word 'proud' very much from those around me. Thank you for believing in me. I do look forward to creating my own path. Maybe I will try to help people in the world, like Daniel did, and you are doing now. Maybe there are teens who struggle with the same kinds of things I do, and I would be able to really understand and empathize with them. Maybe there are other Koreans trying to fit into an environment where they are always considered different. Maybe there are people who come from families where there is physical abuse, and I can help them deal with the pain. I dunno. Some days I know I should just be a teenager and not worry too much about the future. I am a grasshopper, anyway, right?"

"Yep, you are a grasshopper." *He smiled.*

"What is going to happen next? What am I supposed to do during the summer without these sessions? What am I going to do without some psychobabbly thoughts?"

"Hope, that is the great part about your progress. You can have as many psychobabbly thoughts as you want all by yourself."

"I know, cause I am 'centered' and 'self-actualized' right?" *I said goofily.*

"Nice try. Have you ever heard me use words like that? You are where you need to be right now, which is a teenager in transition."

"Yeah, I know. But seriously, what about next year? Are you going to call me Grasshopper in the halls? Am I going to come to any more sessions?"

"Have you told your mother about our sessions yet?"

"Nope, but I have a whole three months to do that if I want you to call me Grasshopper in the halls next year, right?"

He smiled. "Ok, come back next year and tell me you have, and we will discuss any nicknames at that point. As far as next year and counseling sessions, I don't know. I like to reserve counseling for students who are really struggling, but I don't want to have our communication cut off and see your progress stifled in some way. Why don't we meet at the start of next year and decide where to go from there."

"Who knows, maybe by next year I will be a butterfly. Butterflies don't need counseling, right?"

"You will be a butterfly someday, I know it, *he said*. But don't be so fast to outrun this time in your life. Enjoy jumping around from interest to interest, enjoy the transition, and enjoy the natural ups, downs, and even angst which comes from being a teenager. One day, when you are ready, you will shed your cocoon, open your beautiful wings, and bring joy to those around you and to the world. A poetic verse which I believe relates, is part of Ecclesiastes 3:3-4, 'A time to tear down and a time to build, a time to weep and a time to laugh, a time to mourn and a time to dance.' I believe that you will know the right time to spread your wings."

"Thank you, Mr. Morris, for believing in me and for all of your encouraging words. On that note, speaking of poetic verses, I wrote you a poem for our final session. I hope you will like it and won't think it is too silly."

"I know it won't be silly. You have a gift."

"Ok, here goes…"

A Message to One Great Counselor

It's hard to say, in one small poem
A long story or two
I'll try to say in five short words
I look up to you.

Not only 'cause you've been great
Or 'cause you've really cared
And not because you've made me laugh
With all the jokes you shared.
Not only 'cause you are so wise
In your heart and mind
Or because you love me
And were so very kind.
Not only 'cause when I did wrong
You still felt love, not hate
But what has made me look to you
Is how you chose your fate.
You chose to follow your own heart
And Him, your staff and rod
Instead of going your own way
You chose to walk with God.
I'm glad because I know that you're
Not leaving me behind
But taking me with every step
And everything you find.
I'm glad for you because this is
The start and not the end
But through all the years I will
Look up to you, my friend.

We both had little tears in our eyes.

"Hope, your poem is beautiful and touching. I wish I knew what to say other than I am so proud of who you are and who you will become. It was my pleasure to spend this time with you."

"Oh, thank you, Mr. Morris. I will miss these sessions, I really will."

"I will too, Hope."

I went up to him and gave him a big hug. He smiled at me as I turned and walked away. I felt sad to leave. Although it has been a struggle, it has definitely been enlightening and truly special. I walked out into the hall and felt a sensation of freedom, knowing that I have so much of my life ahead of me.

Narrator chimed in, "Hope, I could not help but notice that your story has 22 chapters and 300 pages. Is this something I should comment on?"

"Oh Narrator, if I didn't accept you for who you are I would probably be yelling at you right now. Sometimes people have to struggle through a story to find the meaning of it all, as well as what it means to them. Isn't that what the life of a teenager, or a person in general, is all about? Struggling through life to find a meaning and purpose. How about we just leave it at that, agreed?"

"Agreed. One final note, though, who do you want to say 'The End'?"

"How about we say 'The End' together. That is fitting, right?"

"Right."

Hope/Narrator… The End